MAGIC HEIST

A RILEY CRUZ NOVEL: BOOK THREE

L.A. McBRIDE

author@lamcbride.com

Cover and Illustrations by NMT Design Studio

Ebook ISBN: 9781957445182
Paperback ISBN: 978-1-957445-20-5

To Jilleen Dolbeare, who has been an inspiration, a wonderful friend, and an unfailing support. You should probably wait to read this book until you can laugh without feeling like you just lost a knife fight.

NEWSLETTER SIGNUP

Subscribe to my newsletter for updates, announcements, contests, and bonus content: lamcbride.com/newsletter/

FOREWORD

This series takes place in the same world as the Kali James series. Each series can be read independently. Although every effort has been made to avoid major spoilers, the events in this book overlap with those of Kali's series and include some shared details.

CHAPTER 1

"It's about time you got yourself a stripper pole," Bea called over her shoulder. She trailed the two shifters carrying the last section of the enormous pole up four flights of stairs.

One of the men stumbled, while the other coughed to cover his laugh. Neither of them said anything suggestive, though. Dating their boss seemed to have that effect. Men who used to joke and flirt with me when I bartended at the Sundowner now stammered politely and kept their eyes anywhere but on me. It was annoying.

On the bright side, they'd readily agreed to help muscle the metal sections to the top floor of my new headquarters. At Bea's declaration, they were both eyeing it with more enthusiasm.

I hated to burst their bubble. "It's not a stripper pole."

The men exchanged a skeptical look before carrying the last metal section across the room to put it with the others. I'd had to do a lot of sweet talking and make a generous donation to the Friends of Firefighters charity to salvage it. The neighborhood fire station was being renovated, and apparently old-fashioned fire poles were out of vogue. Win for me.

"But it could be," Bea insisted, fluffing her dyed blonde hair and eyeing the stockier of the two shifters like he was an ice cream sundae.

I shrugged. There was no point arguing with her. The second it was installed, she'd be choreographing raunchy routines no matter what I called that pole. I sat the grocery bag on the bar Kali and I fashioned last week from a pile of reclaimed lumber we found on the third floor. It wasn't pretty, but it was functional. When my next job came through, I'd splurge on an upgrade, complete with a sink and running water.

After lining up the bottles of liquor and tomato juice, I tucked the chilled bag of blood into the nearby dorm-sized refrigerator. Then I laid out paper napkins and red plastic cups. One day, I'd have a shelf lined with real drink glasses, but since I refused to wash dishes in the grimy bathroom sink, they'd have to wait.

The stocky shifter cleared his throat. "Do you need anything else, ma'am?"

It took me a full minute to realize he was talking to me. This was getting out of hand. "Riley," I corrected.

He nodded but didn't repeat my name.

"That's everything. Thank you for helping me haul them inside."

The men didn't wait around to see if I had a change of heart.

I dug out the cheap Bluetooth speaker I brought and connected it to my favorite playlist while Bea organized her latest haul of books and magical supplies on my salvaged bookshelf. She'd scored them at an auction for the inventory left at Old World Occult & Curiosities when it went out of business. Since I had plenty of room, we'd set up a witchy library corner. When it came to magic, I could use all the help I could get.

Bea squinted down at the tiny speaker next to the Ouija board on the top shelf. "Does it go any louder?"

"Nah." A cavernous space like this warehouse deserved a full sound system, but until I got paid again, this would have to do.

She patted my arm. "One thing at a time. Someday, you'll get a big fancy stereo system."

"Someday," I agreed, stopping in front of the lone album cover I'd hung on the wall last week. I'd found it in a neighborhood thrift shop that specialized in old vinyl records and tattered movie posters. I ran my finger across the title—*Point of Know Return* by Kansas. It was a popular enough album, but finding it in West Bottoms felt like coming full circle. Back when I lived with my old alpha Carl in Santa Fe, I'd spent countless hours thumbing through the old albums in the pawn shop. This one had been the compass that pointed me to Kansas City all those years ago.

After straightening the album cover, I surveyed the warehouse I'd blown most of my last paycheck on. With its peeling paint, rickety floorboards, and patched ceiling, this level was in better shape than much of the building. Up here, most of the floor was solid, at least, save for a patch of busted boards in the corner. Everyone insisted that gaping hole was a hazard.

I saw it for the opportunity it was.

I peered down the opening to the floor below. "We're gonna need a circular saw to make this bigger." I wondered whether I'd use a saw enough to justify the investment. A quality battery-operated one could come in handy on jobs. I wondered if I could expense it.

Bea frowned—probably at the idea of me armed with a power tool. "You should ask Bennie for help."

Bennie was the only werewolf other than the alpha who sustained eye contact with me these days. In addition to being my frequent karaoke buddy, he was also a skilled carpenter with a garage packed with tools.

"Good idea," I agreed. He'd be able to give me advice on selecting a dual-purpose saw good for both renovation and burglary. Unfortunately, Bennie was working tonight, so it would have to wait.

With one last look at the disassembled pole, Bea leaned in for a hug. "I wish I could stay."

I knew why she couldn't. The Kansas City coven had sent a formal summons to Helen and the girls requiring their attendance at the monthly business meeting tonight. Naturally, Helen told them to kiss her ass. Even though Helen, Bea, Alyce, and Janis hadn't been part of the local coven for decades, the follow-up summons came directly from the governing Witches' Council. And that one they couldn't ignore. They could, however, make the coven regret inviting them. Helen immediately went into combat planning mode, which involved cream-cheese brownies laced with laxatives and punch spiked generously with Alyce's homemade moonshine.

I hugged Bea back. "I want all the juicy details tomorrow." The first Saturday of the month meant homemade blueberry pancakes, thick-sliced bacon, and real maple syrup. Not even Helen's promise of another round of magic aptitude testing could keep me away. The gossip was a bonus.

Bea patted the low-cut top she'd bedazzled this afternoon,

the words "Snitches Get Stitches" dusted in gold glitter across her ample chest. "Oh, you can count on it, sugar." She wore a wicked smile that didn't bode well for the powers-that-be. She squeezed my arm as she passed. "And don't worry so much about the magic. It'll come."

I wasn't so sure. Thus far, I was proving to be a magical dud. After a lifetime of being the runt in the room, you'd think it would be easier to stomach. But when Zara Bellarose removed the block that held back my magic, that first flush of power rocked my foundation. It felt like change. Yet no matter how many simple spells I recited or potions I dutifully mixed under Helen's watchful eyes, nothing happened. I might see magic now, but I still couldn't channel any of it.

I tamped the worries down and walked Bea out. I'd spent twenty-five years as a magical dud and managed just fine. *Better than fine,* I thought, as I stood on the curb admiring the expensive warehouse I'd rented with money I'd earned. Magic or not, things had changed.

Before I made it back inside, Kali and Craig showed up for my Friday-night painting party. It was my latest brainchild—part free labor, part team building. My heist crew was starting to gel, but we had a ways to go before we operated as a team. But there was nothing like physical labor to bond people. Plus, free food and booze were my insurance policy.

Craig was dressed appropriately for painting in standard blue jeans and a t-shirt. Kali's idea of work clothes looked a lot like *Rosie the Riveter* cosplay. She wore high-waisted jeans with a snug denim shirt knotted at her waist, a red and white polka dot bandana holding back her long, curly dark hair. I catcalled as Kali spun in a circle to show off the cute gingham patches she'd sewn on her back pockets.

"Where should I put these?" Craig held up the four gallons of paint he carried as if they weighed nothing.

"Upstairs." I held open the door.

Kali followed Craig up, waiting for me at the top of the stairs. "Just us?"

"Helen and the girls can't make it," I said. "Everyone else should be on their way."

She huffed. "And Mr. Big Shot?" She surveyed the dilapidated space. "What excuse did he make up to get out of this?"

I felt him behind me, even though I hadn't heard him come up the stairs. Volkov stopped with inches between us, his deep voice rolling over my shoulder. "Sorry to disappoint you, Ms. James." He dropped a hand to the small of my back and nudged me further into the room. "I don't make excuses."

I looked between them. Despite coming to a prickly truce, Kali and Max Volkov were hardly friends. Now that Max and I were exploring whatever this thing was between us, Kali guarded my heart with the ferocity of a best friend. She cocked a hand on her hip and stared at him.

"You're going to work?" She scanned him from the shoulders of his charcoal gray bespoke suit down to the tips of his expensive leather shoes. "Like that?"

Volkov eyed her outfit with a raised brow. Then he took off his suit jacket and tossed it on the oversized sectional in the middle of the room. He locked eyes with me as he unbuttoned the cuffs of his crisp white dress shirt and rolled up his sleeves. "Like this." He lost his tie next, those sharp blue eyes never leaving mine. "Are you ready to put me to work?"

The kind of work I was imagining had nothing to do with painting. Heat coiled low in my belly, and Volkov's lips tilted up. That man knew exactly what he was stoking.

"Oh please." Kali pretended to gag. "Get a room."

Dez's arrival cut her commentary short. "I come bearing gifts." He lifted arms loaded with plastic grocery bags before heading for the bar.

I'd put Dez in charge of snacks, and he didn't let me down. He filled the remaining space on the bar with bags of chips, pretzels, and corn nuts, along with two kinds of spicy salsa, guacamole, and a four-layer bean dip that looked homemade. I grabbed his arm as he finished laying out the spread and reeled him in for a bear hug. "You're officially my favorite person."

"I should be," he grumbled. "I gave up my Friday night to help you paint your place." He held up a chip smothered in guac, and I happily accepted his offering.

"Our place," I corrected after I finished chewing. It was our new headquarters, after all. "That reminds me, we need a name." When I sent the invite out via group chat, I'd told everyone to come up with names for our headquarters. I pointed to the stack of paper and rusty coffee can at the end of the bar. So far, the only person who had contributed suggestions was Bea, and from my quick snoop, none of them could be printed on a sign. "I'm giving everyone one week to add their suggestions to the pot. Next week, we're voting."

Dez groaned but scribbled something on a piece of paper, folded it in half, and tossed it in the can.

Nash Mitchell arrived next, an angry rooster tucked under his arm.

"You brought Garth!" I snatched the birdcage from him and sat it on a nearby table.

"I wouldn't let him out if I were you," Nash warned.

I ignored him, unlatching the door to pet Garth's sapphire-blue chest. He crowed triumphantly at Nash before fluffing his feathers and hopping down from the table to explore the room.

Dez crossed his arms and scowled at Nash. "What are you wearing?"

Nash seemed his normal I-just-rolled-out-of-bed grungy self to me. As usual, his clothes looked like he'd rummaged them out of a laundry pile. Thanks to Kali's recent makeover for our last job, Nash's dark blonde hair was short and stylish, but scruff already covered his jaw again. I didn't understand Dez's jab until Kali gasped and rushed over to stare down at Nash's feet.

"Are those," her voice cracked, "Crocs?"

They were indeed. In Kali's book, those were a fashion sin that ranked right up there with my favorite heist fanny pack.

Nash scowled. "I didn't have a choice." He pointed at Garth, who was circling the bar as if gauging the best way to get to the food spread on top of it. "That menace shits in my shoes every chance he gets. These are easy to hose off."

"I'm sure he doesn't mean to," I tried.

Volkov's rumbling laugh made Nash clench his jaw. "He means to. He ruined my favorite pair of cowboy boots and all of my runners."

I reached into my pocket and pulled out the gift Helen sent for Nash. "I guess that explains this."

Nash took the bracelet from me and held it up to the light. He examined the small charm dangling from the delicate silver chain. "Is this triangle some kind of powerful witch symbol?"

"It's supposed to be a poop emoji." I grinned. "Alyce's idea." According to Alyce, a poop-be-gone charm required an appropriate symbol to be effective. I was pretty sure she was pulling my leg, but what did I know? I was hardly a magical powerhouse.

Everyone studied the bracelet. If you squinted, you could see the shape better.

"And it'll work?" Nash asked.

"One way to find out," I said.

When Nash lunged for Garth, causing the poor bird to squawk and flap his wings aggressively, I stepped between them. "I'll do it." I made soothing noises as I fastened the little bracelet around Garth's leg, right above his wicked-looking spur. He preened, holding his leg out for everyone to admire. I petted his chest feathers and cooed. "Aren't you a pretty boy?"

Kali scrunched her nose and peered at Garth's fluffy butt. "Where does it go? The poop, I mean."

I shrugged. "You'd have to ask Helen or Alyce." As long as it wasn't on my floor or in my shoes, I didn't care where it went.

Before I could distribute paint brushes and put everyone to work, my phone vibrated in my pocket. I answered without looking.

"Video call in half an hour," Kage Sato said without preamble. "You'll need to see this."

CHAPTER 2

Thirty minutes was plenty of time to pour a round of drinks while Dez hooked up the giant flat screen and small camera he'd ordered. By the time the video call connected, we were sprawled out on my comfy new sectional, anticipating our next fat payday.

Despite the Pokémon Charizard shirt he wore, Kage Sato was all business. "Be ready to leave Monday." He stood next to a wall-sized screen that made Dez's eyes glaze with envy.

Before Dez could derail the conversation by demanding specs, I jumped in. "Where are we going?" I was half afraid Sato wouldn't be able to tell me what I needed to steal or where I'd find it. It wouldn't be the first time the Enclave sent me after a demon relic without a description or location. If it became a habit, I'd have to renegotiate my fee to account for the annoyance.

The camera Dez set up had a wide-angle lens that gave Sato a view of most of the room. Even on video, Sato's dark eyes were unnerving as he took stock of my team while we waited for him to deliver our next assignment.

He frowned. "Are you having a party?"

I followed his gaze to the bar behind us. Between the abandoned warehouse aesthetic, the leftover snacks, and the half-empty drinks in cheap red plastic cups, it looked more like a teenage kegger than team building. I lifted my glass. "Sure am." Unlike the cocktails I mixed for everyone else, mine held strawberry-flavored water since I wasn't much of a drinker. I chugged it anyway and set the empty cup on the coffee table. "So, what's the job?"

Sato's frown deepened, and he pointed behind me. "Is that a rooster?"

I spun around. Sure enough, Garth was strutting across the bar top, his little chest puffed with accomplishment. I moved to shoo him off. Before I reached him, he kicked Dez's Bloody Mary over, the blood-thickened cocktail spilling on the bar and dripping down the side. I lunged for Garth, but not before he buried his beak in the pooling liquid and hoovered up some O positive.

"Gross!" I ignored his angry squawking as I scooped him off the bar. "We don't drink blood," I admonished before setting him on the floor. He immediately circled around behind the bar, looking for a good launch point. "A little help here," I called.

I grabbed a handful of paper napkins to mop up the mess. Dez saved the snacks while Nash attempted to herd Garth away from the bar. Garth dodged his first attempt, so Nash crowded the rooster against the wall and dove for him. Garth waited until Nash almost reached him before darting to one side and plucking a hair from Nash's head for a trophy. I clapped my hand over my mouth to keep the laugh from bubbling out.

Dez didn't attempt to hide his amusement, clutching his

side as he laughed. Nash gritted his teeth and glared at Dez as he pushed himself to his feet.

When Volkov chuckled, Nash snapped. "If you think it's so damn easy, why don't you try?"

Chasing a rooster was so far out of Max Volkov's wheelhouse, it wasn't even funny. But the man was an alpha, and a challenge was a challenge. Volkov rolled his shoulders and cracked his knuckles, letting a growl build in his chest as he stalked closer to us.

I bit my lip. Somehow, I didn't think intimidation was the way to go with a rooster.

Garth tilted his little head and watched Volkov approach, his red eyes lit with unholy interest. As soon as Garth caught sight of Volkov's fancy leather shoes, it was on. He flew at the man in a rage of flapping wings and sharp spurs, crowing his victory as he attacked the expensive Italian leather with zeal. I'd never seen Volkov back down from anything or anyone, but he scrambled out of Garth's warpath. Volkov's eyes widened, and he caught himself before he retreated more than a few steps. Although Volkov eventually managed a firm hold on the rooster, Garth left bloody gashes down both of his forearms. I reached for Garth before he could inflict permanent damage.

After plenty of petting and soothing, Garth settled enough I could put him down on the floor. Not trusting him to stay put, I snatched the liquor bottles off the bar and carried them with me for safekeeping. The last thing I needed was booze-soaked floorboards. I put the bottles on the coffee table and plopped back on the couch, thankful I'd sprung for stain guard. With Garth in residence, I'd need it. I settled against the cushion, a disgruntled Volkov sitting beside me.

"Now, what's the job?" I asked again.

Sato snapped his mouth closed and shook his head, as if clearing it before stepping to the side. He pointed a remote at the oversized screen. "Watch."

The video wasn't what I expected. Instead of surveillance footage, it was a national celebrity gossip show. A pretty woman with sleek dark hair stood outside a brightly lit home with crisp modern architecture and enough windows to see the people milling inside. "In an industry of excess," she said, "Monty Corville's parties have gained a reputation for hedonistic thrills."

The footage shifted to a wobbly cell phone video that panned a backyard full of drunk revelers gazing up at a naked man balanced precariously on a balcony railing. He was blonde and leanly muscled, a strategically placed blur the only thing preventing a full-frontal view.

The man was holding court. He smiled and revved up the crowd until their chant of "jump, jump, jump" was deafening. Then he held his arms out wide, spun around as graceful as a ballerina, and dove off the balcony without hesitation, his body arcing toward the swimming pool below. From the camera angle, it looked like he would hit the concrete, but he cleared the edge and plunged under water. As if that were a cue, people splashed in after him, letting out a raucous cheer when he surfaced.

Kali leaned close and whispered. "I don't get it."

I didn't get it either.

Sato hit pause, the daredevil's face center screen. I leaned forward for a closer look. There was something off about the man's expression. Although his smile was easy and his body relaxed, his dark eyes appeared flat.

"Who is he?" Nash asked.

But that wasn't the right question. I stood and moved closer. "He's not human, is he?"

"We're not sure," Sato admitted. "He could be human, but based on what I'm about to show you, he could be a supernatural." He tapped the screen. "Meet Monty Corville. He's a stuntman who has built a reputation for wild parties and no-holds-barred stunt work since he popped up on the Hollywood scene six months ago. He's currently working on a big-budget action movie. Until this video surfaced, he wasn't even on our radar."

"And now that he is?" Craig asked, sharing a loaded look with Volkov. As the enforcer for the Interior Territory, Craig knew better than most the penalties for exposing our kind to humans. If Monty Corville was a supernatural and he was connected with a demon artifact, he was drawing far too much attention to himself.

"We'll get to that, but he's not what we're after." Sato zoomed in on the antique library table in the background. Nestled beneath a bank of windows overlooking the city skyline, the table held a single object under a locked display case.

I eyed the old book beneath the glass case. "I'm guessing that's not a dictionary."

"It is not," Sato said. "That is a demon book of spells we've been trying to track down for years."

"And it happened to turn up on a Hollywood gossip show?" Nash asked skeptically.

Volkov tipped his chin in agreement. "A little too convenient. How do we know it's not a trap?"

Their paranoia was a stretch. Ever since Zara Bellarose attacked me, Volkov and Nash saw threats to my safety lurking in every shadow.

I patted both their knees. "If someone was going to lay a trap for us, California doesn't seem the best place to do it." California was a long way from Kansas City. No way could someone predict we'd go after it. I certainly wasn't the only one hunting demon artifacts. And as I learned on the last job, I wasn't even the only retrieval specialist on the Enclave's payroll.

Volkov scowled at Nash's denim-clad knee before stretching his arm along the couch, his fingers brushing my shoulder.

Garth picked that moment to make his move. He landed gracefully on the coffee table and dropped a wing, circling a bottle with single-minded purpose.

Sato watched with growing fascination. "Is he trying to mate with that tequila bottle?"

"He's not very bright," Nash muttered.

I elbowed him. "He's lonely." I rescued the bottle from Garth's misguided attention. Then I bribed Garth with a handful of barbecue corn nuts I tossed behind the couch. "Okay, back to the job. I'm assuming you want us to retrieve the book of demon spells?"

Sato watched us for a minute before regaining his composure. "Correct. We also need to know if Corville stumbled on the book and thought it was a pretty collectible." He pointed to the glass display case. "The fact that he has it out in the open during a party suggests he might not have a clue what is in his possession."

"If he does?" Volkov asked, his body tensing next to mine.

Sato flicked the remote, so the video continued playing in the background. Monty Corville worked the crowd like a pro, accepting slaps on the back and high fives as if they were his due. "If he does, he needs to be taken out."

"As in—" Dez drew his finger across his throat and made a gurgling sound.

Sato inclined his head. "Yes. If Corville is a supernatural, and he's recklessly flaunting that demon spell book, the Enclave has authorized elimination of the target."

Volkov swore. "And who do you expect to take out this man? Riley?"

Murder-for-hire was definitely not in my job description.

Before Volkov could continue raging, Sato cut in. "Of course not. All Riley and her team need to do is determine whether Corville is human or a vampire or other supernatural. I'll have a Shadow waiting for the kill order."

"Who?" Volkov demanded.

"You know I can't tell you that," Sato said.

Volkov clenched his jaw. "It's too risky. Stealing that book is one thing, but sending her in to cozy up to Corville and ask dangerous questions could get her killed."

"Hey." I leaned closer. "It's not like I'd ask him outright if he's a vamp. I can be subtle."

I looked to my team to back me up. Nash coughed into his fist, and Dez grimaced. *Jerks.* Volkov kept glaring at Sato.

Sato gestured toward Nash and Dez. "She'll have backup."

"Not good enough," Volkov snarled.

Both men stiffened at his easy dismissal. *So much for team bonding.*

I put a hand on Volkov's arm. "We'll be careful, Max."

Volkov stared at Craig, who nodded, some type of unspoken communication passing between them. "Send Ward," Volkov said. At one time, both Craig and Volkov had served as Shadows—the supernatural equivalent of assassins and spies—themselves.

Sato considered him. "If you go, it's as a Shadow, not his enforcer. You answer to me."

Neither Volkov nor Craig looked happy about it, but neither argued.

"Understood," Craig said.

"Good. It's settled." Sato looked at Craig. "Securing the spell book is our priority. You know the routine, Ward. Unless I give the order, you're on standby only. Stay off set. Got it?"

Craig gave a curt nod.

Sato closed the video and pulled up a still image on the screen with a California driver's license. "We've taken the liberty of creating a fake identity for you." The license listed Riley Arnold and sported a photo of me grinning at the camera. Keeping my first name was a smart move, since it reduced the chances of slipping up.

"I take it this isn't a snatch and grab then," I said.

"It's not. Until you determine the extent of Monty Corville's knowledge, you'll be embedded with the staff, but you need to work fast. This is a national media story. Chances are, we aren't the only ones who spotted that book. Be prepared for other interested parties to go after it."

The familiar buzz of excitement built, and I leaned forward. "What's my cover?"

Sato pulled up the cast list and pointed to a woman with a no-nonsense ponytail and a compact build. "It so happens that a position opened up when a female stunt double had an unfortunate accident that landed her in a cast." The way he said accident made me wonder if the Enclave orchestrated it.

Poor woman.

"I'll be working directly with Corville?" I asked.

"Not quite," Sato said. "You'll be working on a different

movie but at the same studio. That should give you enough access to Corville to determine whether he's a vampire."

"Let me get this straight," I said. "You want me to perform death-defying stunts and pretend to be a Hollywood action hero while stealing a dangerous book of demon spells?"

"Yes," Sato agreed.

I folded my hands behind my head and leaned back. "I'm in."

Basking in California weather, rubbing elbows with movie stars, and charging fresh seafood to the Enclave? This was shaping up to be the best job ever. From the buzz of conversation around me, I wasn't the only one excited about an undercover Hollywood gig. Everyone but Volkov, anyway.

"There's one more thing." Sato waited until he had our full attention to shatter my good mood. "I thought you should know. The Enclave released Zara Bellarose."

Silence blanketed the room. Volkov was the first to react, standing as if he wanted to lunge through the screen. "What do you mean, released?"

Sato's eye twitched. "She claimed she'd merely acquired a set of valuable artifacts as a collector and that she had no idea what they did."

"That's bullshit," I argued. "She used the Cuffs of Valac to control Isaac."

Craig crossed his big arms over his chest and glared at Sato. "And she used that witch to attack Kali, so she could get her hands on a dangerous blood-tracing spell."

Isaac had used a retrieval spell to yank it out of Kali's head, injuring her in the process. Armed with that blood-tracing spell, Bellarose could trace any bloodline. I had no idea what she planned to use it for, but I was certain whatever it was wouldn't be good.

"Why on earth would they let her go?" I asked Sato. The Enclave had sent me after the relic in the first place. They knew exactly how dangerous those cuffs were, not to mention the blood-tracing spell. Why let Bellarose go, knowing what she'd used them for? According to Sato, they'd given the green light to take out Monty Corville for far less.

Sato looked away. "Without Isaac or Luca Cardelli to testify, there was no evidence to contradict her claim." Luca Cardelli was the original retrieval specialist tasked with bringing in the artifact before he double-crossed the Enclave and gave it to Bellarose.

"Since when does the Enclave require evidence?" Volkov's fists clenched at his sides. "What's their end game here?" he demanded, not taking his eyes off Sato.

Sato's expression blanked. "That's above both our pay grades. All I can tell you is that as of last week, Zara Bellrose was a free witch."

CHAPTER 3

Kali would forgive me almost anything. Leaving her behind while I spent the week on a Hollywood set was not on that list. Despite it being her busy season at the costume shop, she assured me her help could run it in her absence. Because Craig was now coming with us, he didn't even try to talk her out of it. He wasn't thrilled that Sato banned him from working on the set with us, though. As a Shadow, the job required him to be incognito until the strike was called in. Craig Ward was a 6'2" wall of muscle with flint-colored eyes and a shaved head. The only place he'd blend in was a prison yard.

I shoved my frustration over Bellarose's release aside and focused on what I could control. Because Sato only secured an identity for me, I asked Dez to hack into the studio employment database and add Kali and Nash. The costume department for the film was tight-knit, but thanks to Dez's online mojo, one of the junior costume staff members suddenly found herself on mandatory jury duty, leaving an opening Kali was more than happy to fill. Dez added Nash to the security staff, which would give him access to places off limits to the rest of us. Although I floated the idea of Dez taking over a cameraman spot, he preferred to work off site. He booked us a swanky vacation rental on the Enclave's dime that promised great Wi-Fi, hillside views in Silver Lake, and reasonably close proximity to the filming location.

Once we had our identities sorted, Volkov offered to arrange a chartered flight that would have us in Los Angeles by Sunday afternoon. When I hugged him goodbye, he leaned in, brushing the shell of my ear with his lips. "Don't forget," he rumbled. "I'm looking forward to tomorrow."

As if I could forget our first official date.

By the time the party broke up, we were all buzzing with anticipation for the week ahead. As usual, Dez was the last to leave, helping me put away food and toss the empty cups. The third time he gave me the side eye while running his hand through his ruffled red hair, I gave him my full attention. "What's up?"

"We should sit." He dropped to the couch and patted the seat next to him.

Based on his somber expression, this wasn't about the job. I battled my nerves, tucking a leg underneath me before turning to face him. "What did you find?"

"It's about your mom." He paused when I flinched. At my half-hearted smile, he continued. "Now that we have her real last name, I did some digging."

When I'd found out that the woman who raised me wasn't my biological mother, I'd taken it like the sucker punch it was. After weeks of letting the knowledge settle in, the wound was still raw inside my chest. "And?" My voice came out steadier than I felt.

"On the surface, Amelia Hunt had an idyllic middle-class

upbringing in upstate New York. Her father was an insurance salesman, and her mother taught high school art classes. Your mom—Amelia," he corrected himself.

"My mom," I insisted. DNA match or not, she'd always be my mother. She'd been the one to kiss my scrapes and bruises. She'd celebrated my first steps. And every night, she regaled me with bedtime stories about a girl named Mel who went on the most fantastical globe-trotting adventures. My stomach knotted as I remembered the way my mother's eyes lit up as she told them, her voice a whisper in the dark. We didn't have many books—or much of anything—when I was growing up, but she hadn't need them. She knew those stories by heart, and I'd listened to them so many times that now so did I.

"Are they still alive?" I asked. "Amelia's parents?"

Dez shook head. "No. I'm sorry. I couldn't find any living relatives."

Unlike my mother whose DNA we were able to run from a hair sample, I had nothing of my father. There was no way to track his true identity down or even to know if he was my biological father. For a second, I entertained the idea of using the blood-tracing spell Bellarose stole from Kali's memory to track down any living relatives. But that spell was fueled by blood magic, and if the past few months taught me anything, it was how dangerous and unpredictable demon spells could be.

"It's just me, then." I swallowed and let the idea go. "What else did you discover about my mom?"

Dez squeezed my hand. "Your mom was a good student, placed in the gifted program in elementary school. She took dance and gymnastics classes from the time she was four. Based on the competitive records I found, she excelled on the balance beam and parallel bars."

Why had she never mentioned that? I frowned and stared at my hands, twisting the copper and silver ring she left for me around my finger. *Why hadn't she told me anything about her childhood?* Despite living with her for the first twelve years of my life, there was so much I didn't know. And discovering it secondhand like this hollowed me out in a way I hadn't expected.

I searched for remnants of the activities she loved in my memories. Thinking back, I recalled the graceful way she danced out of my father's reach after she'd sprayed him while washing the dishes. I saw hints of it in the way she never wobbled when she climbed on the counters to reach a higher shelf. She shared it through the cartwheels and back handsprings she taught me how to do in our backyard.

I blinked against the tears and the scratch in my throat. "You said on the surface she had an idyllic middle-class upbringing. What did you mean?" My pulse sped up as I ran through all the ways a picture-perfect life could be rotten underneath its pretty trappings. People didn't assume an alias and move across the country without something chasing them. I should know.

"The further I dug, the more anomalies I discovered." Dez turned the flat screen back on and reached for his keyboard. "When Amelia turned sixteen, she abruptly stopped competing." He pulled up gymnastics' results, scrolling through a long list punctuated by her name at regular intervals until the year she turned sixteen.

"That's not unusual, though. Lots of kids outgrow an interest. She could have discovered boys or got a part-time job," I reasoned.

"Maybe. But she transferred to a new school around the

same time—right after she got her driver's license." Dez clicked to a photo of her license.

I was unprepared for the glimpse of my mother as a teenager, the flash of grief stealing my breath. The photo of her as a young woman was both achingly familiar and a complete stranger. Her features were softer, her cheeks rounder, and her face flushed with youth.

"Her eyes." I pressed a palm against the ache building in my chest. "But I have her eyes," I whispered, trying to make sense of the soulful brown gaze staring back at me.

Not even the DNA results hit me like this. A single crappy DMV photo ripped away the one thing that proved we shared more than fractured memories. The vivid blue eyes that I knew better than my own were gone, and in their place was someone else.

Dez scooted closer to me, his face pinched with concern. "Are you alright?"

I nodded, the lump in my throat making it difficult to speak. When I wrestled control of my emotions again, I touched the screen. "She must have worn contacts during my entire childhood, so we'd look more alike." *But why?* Since finding out we weren't blood relation, I'd run through a dozen scenarios. *Maybe I was adopted. Or maybe my mother died in childbirth, or she ran out on my father. Maybe Amelia was my stepmother.* None of those scenarios required us to have the same eye color, though. "You said she changed schools?" I asked.

"She did." Dez pulled up a photo of a beautiful modern high school nestled among trees and well-manicured grounds. "The private school she'd attended prior to her move was one of the best in the state, known for its gifted and talented program." He opened her high school transcript next. "At the private school, she'd taken a broad range of college prep courses including advanced physics, computer engineering, and calculus."

I whistled. "Impressive."

"Exactly." Dez opened a second high school home page. "Which is why it's weird that she went from that to this." Lincoln Vo-Tech billed itself as an alternative high school that gave at-risk youth practical job skills and boasted a dismal sixty-nine percent graduation rate. The home page showed an old, depressing industrial-looking building with minimal windows and an empty parking lot. The webpage listed the range of career pathways the school offered—everything from auto repair to certified nursing assistant training. Quotes touting hands-on experience and job placement appeared alongside photos of several bored-looking students.

"Did her family fall on hard times?" I asked.

Dez shook his head. "No. In fact, her father got a big pay raise around the same time. He moved from selling insurance to investigating insurance fraud. Plus, her mother worked at the school, so they got free tuition for Amelia."

"Why would that be a pay raise for her father?" It seemed to me like there was a lot more money in insurance sales than investigations.

"For one, he didn't investigate petty fraud," Dez said. "He went after big-time swindlers—people who filed claims on multi-million-dollar properties and rare art and antiques. His salary almost doubled in the year after the job change."

I frowned. That didn't make sense. Why would a straight-A student transfer from a private college prep high school to a crumbling school that catered to at-risk students if it wasn't about money? "She might have wanted to pursue nursing or another career field that required more hands-on training," I theorized. There were plenty of blue-collar jobs that paid well and required an aptitude for math and science.

"If that were the case, I'd expect her to have taken classes in a single career path." Dez pulled up her transcript. "But that's not what she did."

I scanned the list. There was no rhyme or reason to her class selections. She'd taken several welding classes. Given her metal-working skills as a jewelry maker, those made the most sense. However, she'd also taken building design and construction, a couple HVAC classes, a course on electrical engineering principles, several computer classes, one on civil engineering, and a class on the installation of fire alarms of all things. I looked at Dez. "Okay. That's odd."

He nodded. "Around this time, she also landed in some trouble."

I pictured my mom with her soft voice and sunny smile and tried to imagine her as a rebellious teenager. I couldn't manage it. "What kind of trouble?"

"Two months after starting at her new high school, she was arrested along with a friend for possession of stolen goods. Because she didn't have a record, she got off with community service."

"What about the friend?"

Dez showed me a mugshot of a young man with hard eyes and a smug smile. He reminded me of the young men in Carl's pack. He looked to be about the same age as Amelia, but there was no doubt he was bad news.

"The friend was Dirk O'Malley, and despite being the suspect in the robbery, he walked out of the precinct shortly after being brought in. All charges against him were dropped." Dez glanced at me to gauge how I was taking the news.

"Dirk?" I sneered. *What kind of name was Dirk?* I scowled at the dark-haired man on the screen. "Robbery was the more serious of the two charges. Why let him walk? It doesn't make sense."

"It does when you realize the O'Malleys are an organized crime family with deep pockets and a shark for a lawyer," Dez countered.

I rolled my neck to ease the kink that was forming. "Okay, so this Dirk O'Malley got her involved in his petty crimes and then left her to deal with the fallout." Even in a crappy police photo, O'Malley radiated bad boy vibes. I could see how that would appeal to a sheltered good girl from the right side of the tracks. It was practically a teenage rite of passage to taste the danger that came wrapped in leather and cheap cologne. "Is that why she ran? To get away from him?"

Dez grimaced. "Not exactly."

I waited for him to elaborate.

Instead of flipping through more files, he turned to me. "As far as I can tell, they parted ways. But that was the first of several arrests for your mother." Dez's face softened with sympathy as he ticked off her crimes. "There were a couple petty larceny charges as a teen, but the big one came years after she was involved with Dirk O'Malley." He paused as if he was gauging how I was handling the news.

"Out with it," I said.

"At twenty-six, she was arrested for one of the biggest art heists on the east coast."

My mouth dropped open. "What the hell, Dez?"

He sat the remote aside and met my eyes. "She might not be your biological mother, but it appears you inherited your criminal tendencies from her."

I kneaded the knots in my shoulders. *My mother, a thief?* I couldn't reconcile that image with the woman I'd known. "How did she not serve hard time?"

"Bail was set at two million dollars and was posted anonymously the day it was set," Dez said.

"O'Malley?"

"Nah. Dirk O'Malley was shot in the back of the head by his cousin a couple years prior."

"Then who?" I asked. Her middle-class parents wouldn't have been able to scrounge together that kind of money.

Dez shrugged. "No idea, but she never showed up for her trial. After that, there was no trace of her. Whoever bailed her out made sure Amelia Hunt no longer existed."

CHAPTER 4

"Put your back into it," Helen urged as the potion bomb Janis lobbed at my head fell short.

A couple hours ago when Helen pitched the idea over brunch, it seemed fun. Instead of entertaining me with stories of the girls going toe-to-toe with the coven, they'd been uncharacteristically subdued over bacon and pancakes. Since they changed the subject when I asked about the coven meeting, I assumed it hadn't gone well. So, when Helen suggested a magical gauntlet, I'd agreed. Because magical dodgeball made a huge mess, we'd chosen to do it outside rather than destroy Helen's living room.

Of course, Helen made it sound like one of those fun obstacle course mud runs where you get a Viking hat at the end, except with witches. What started as a way to test my magical ability—which thus far was non-existent—quickly turned into a free-for-all that had me ducking the barrage of potion bombs Helen, Alyce, Janis, and Bea pelted me with. The ones that missed their mark exploded with all manner of nasty magic. There were flash bombs, glitter bombs, and Helen's latest invention, the smoke snake.

On impact, a demonic snake made of billowing smoke that reeked of sulfur rose from the busted shell. The snake's hell-fire eyes tracked my movements like a sentient creature, lava venom dripping from obscenely long fangs. It was freaking terrifying. *I should have known better than to tell Helen about Bellarose's snakes.* The only one cursing Helen's creation more than me was Bea who harbored a healthy fear of snakes.

Despite being in her seventies, Helen possessed wicked aim, and unlike the other three witches, most of hers struck true. The welts on my legs and torso were evidence. And yet, not a single one that struck me released their magic.

After shaking a couple and testing a few more by tossing them at Bea, Helen narrowed her eyes on me. Then she loaded up the deep pockets of her cardigan and doubled down, hurling bombs at me like a major league pitcher. With every magic bomb that hit me, Helen's frown deepened.

Finally, I held up my hands in front of me. "Uncle," I yelled. I was covered in debris and had a bruise the size of a grape-fruit on my left side where I'd taken repeated hits.

Helen reluctantly lowered the potion ball she clutched and exchanged a look with Alyce.

"You must be getting old," Bea taunted Helen. "Most of those were duds."

With a scowl, Helen pulled a mud-colored ball out of her pocket and slammed it against Bea's thigh. Bea yelped and scrambled away while trying to brush the spell remnants off her leg. "Damn it, Helen. What did you do that for?" Bea danced from foot to foot until the spell ran its course.

"Ants-in-your-pants?" Alyce guessed.

Helen nodded.

I pointed at the busted potion balls littering the ground. "If those aren't duds, why don't they work on me?"

Helen and Alyce exchanged another loaded look.

"Go on. Spit it out." I crossed my arms over my chest. After Dez's drama bomb about my mother's secret life as a high-end art thief, whatever it was probably wouldn't even be the worst news this week.

Instead of answering, Helen handed me what was left of her stash. "Here. You try."

Because I wasn't dumb enough to toss Helen's own potion ball back at her, I threw a glitter ball at the side of the house. Nothing. The flash bomb I threw next was equally disappointing.

Helen's brow furrowed. "What I don't understand is why they worked for you before but not now."

Alyce tilted her head and studied me. "Whatever Zara Bellarose did to unlock Riley's magic must have caused this."

I thought back to the potion balls Helen had armed me with in the past. "I don't think so. At Damien Creed's auction, both Dez and I tossed your potion balls into that basement, but only his went off. The ones I threw were duds." When Helen narrowed her eyes at the insult to her magical arsenal, I corrected myself. "At least they seemed like duds."

"What about the ones you used on Bellarose?" Helen asked. "They all worked, right?"

"I don't think the incognito bomb did. Bellarose was able to see me fine." I frowned. "But I know the flash bomb worked."

"Why would one work but not the others?" Bea asked.

I mentally walked through the confrontation with Bellarose again. Something had to be different, but what? Then it hit me. "When I threw the flash bomb, I was wearing gloves. All the rest, I touched." I slumped into a nearby patio chair. "That must be it."

"I'll grab gloves, so we can test it," Janis called over her shoulder as she disappeared inside Helen's side of the tangerine-colored duplex she shared with Bea. The other three witches joined me at the table. When Janis returned, she carried a pair of stretchy gloves, a pitcher of ice-cold lemonade, and homemade sugar cookies.

When I reached for a cookie, Helen swatted my hand. "Test first."

"Fine," I grumbled, slipping the gloves on before tossing the last of the glitter balls at the ground. This one detonated fine, spreading rainbow glitter all over Helen's orthopedic sneakers. I grimaced. "Sorry."

With a huff, Helen handed over a cookie. The sugar rush was exactly what I needed. I shoved it in my mouth and reached for a second while I waited for Helen to spill whatever she was holding back.

"We can't be sure," she started. "But Alyce and I have a working theory."

"Which is?" I prompted, dusting the crumbs off my shirt.

Helen looked around as if she was afraid someone was listening. "We need to do another test before I hazard a guess."

I dropped my head to the table with a thunk. Max Volkov was picking me up for our date in a couple hours. At this rate, I'd be a mass of bruises for it. *Sexy.*

Helen patted my leg. "One more test. You're not a typical witch, hon. But I don't want to jump to dangerous conclusions until I've gathered enough information."

I lifted my head. "Dangerous?"

Alyce handed me another cookie in a blatant distraction

attempt. "Eat up, Riley. You're going to need your energy for the ward gauntlet."

When it was apparent Helen wouldn't budge until I'd jumped through all the magical hoops she'd set up, I finished my cookie. It went down like sawdust, clogging my throat. I took another gulp of lemonade before jumping to my feet. I looked at Helen and then at Alyce, who—despite her smile—was nervously twisting her apron between her fingers. "Let's get this over with because I'm not leaving here until one of you tells me what has you both so worried."

We moved inside, where they'd set wards in the basement. I opened the door leading downstairs and saw the patchwork of magic. Some wards blanketed the doors and windows, while others crisscrossed the floor in an intricate web. Each of them pulsed with power.

I studied the magical gauntlet while the girls crowded behind me. "And none of you can see the wards?"

"Not a one," Alyce assured me.

Apparently, the ability to see magic was rare. But without the ability to wield it, it wasn't doing me much good.

"The ones closest to us are the simplest," Helen explained. "You've got your basic repulsion wards on the stairs, then a few zingers at the bottom." She pointed toward the large unfinished room where boxes were stacked haphazardly among discarded furniture. "The remainder of the room has wards meant to incapacitate interlopers. One touch should knock you on your butt. And over there," Helen indicated the small window on the far wall, "well the one blocking the window should lay you out for the better part of a day if you breach it."

"I have a date," I objected.

Bea patted me on the back. "Sorry, sweetie, but we need to know."

I cracked my knuckles and rolled my neck. *Might as well get this over with.* "And I'm supposed to find a way around them?"

"Not around them," Helen said. "I want you to walk through them."

So, I did. The magic bent around my body as I passed. I saw the wards, felt them like static electricity brushing against my skin. There was no resistance, no repercussions as I walked straight through them.

When I wiggled my hand through the strongest ward, I shot the girls a triumphant look that faltered when I spotted the slump of Helen's shoulders. "This isn't the first ward I've walked through, you know. Why do you look so worried?"

"Let's go upstairs," Helen said. "We'll tell you about our theory and about our summons to the coven meeting."

I trudged after them, mentally preparing myself for the disappointment of hearing them confirm what I already knew. There might be a witch in my family tree, but I only inherited a trickle of power. Watching other people wield magic was almost worse than not seeing it at all.

When we reached the living room, I waited in tense silence, watching as Helen and Alyce looked anywhere but at me. "It's not that bad. In my line of work, walking through wards comes in handy." I shrugged. "So what if I don't have powerful magic?"

Bea put an arm around me and squeezed.

Helen drew her shoulders back and perched on the couch across from me. "Power isn't the issue, hon. That you have in spades."

I looked around at their solemn faces. "I don't understand." Over the last few weeks, they'd watched me try and fail at all kinds of magical tasks. "We just established that I have the magical equivalent of cooties. Touching Helen's potion bombs rendered them useless. That's the opposite of powerful." I pointed at Alyce and Helen. "One of you needs to explain this theory."

Alyce stood up abruptly and left the room. When she came back, she carried a mason jar full of moonshine and five shot glasses. She poured a generous amount in each and passed them out. I declined, but she placed the glass in my hand, anyway. "You're gonna need that, sweetheart."

After downing our shots, Helen grabbed a tattered book from the end table, flipped it open, and plopped it into my lap. She tapped on an entry halfway down the page.

I started to read out loud. "Most witches can work small amounts of magic from each of the elements—earth, air, water, and fire. A fortunate few can harness a single element on a deeper level. These witches are known as elementals. Earth elementals are the most common and fire the rarest." This was all common knowledge.

"Keep reading," Helen instructed.

"Rarer still are the witches who are immune to elemental magic, known as nulls. Nulls disrupt and dampen the magic around them, walking unscathed through wards and elemental attacks. Because of this rare power, nulls have been used by other supernaturals as a shield against magic." I looked up. "Why have I never heard of this?"

Helen gestured toward the girls. "Because we've never seen a null in our lifetimes. They were thought to have died out a couple generations ago."

"And you think I'm a null?"

Alyce and Helen both nodded. Bea and Janis didn't seem surprised, so they must have discussed this theory.

Bea sighed. "It would explain why compulsion and alpha commands don't work on you, Riley."

"And this." I tapped the sepia goat head tattoo on the inside of my wrist—a tattoo created with magical ink. If I were a null, it would also explain why mine was funky body art while Kali's crow tattoo held powerful magic. Not that I was complaining on that front. *Better a dud tattoo than a demon tethered to my soul.*

I stared down at the book in my lap. "Okay. Now what?"

"Now, we keep this to ourselves," Helen said, her voice sharp, "and we keep you out of the coven's clutches."

Janis flipped her long red braid over her shoulder and reached around me for the moonshine. "That's easier said than done since the coven ordered us to deliver Riley to them for a magical evaluation and training."

I groaned. I'd had enough magical evaluation. Plus, the Kansas City coven included a bunch of uptight witches who loved their rules almost more than their magic. They'd also been at odds with Helen and the girls since they left the coven decades ago.

Helen glared at Janis. "That's not going to happen. If they find out Riley is a null," Helen warned, "they'll lock her down in the name of training, so no one can use her against them. She doesn't need their brand of training. She's got her instincts, and she's got us."

I snapped my head up. "What do you mean lock down?"

Alyce tipped her chin. "You don't worry about that. We'll take care of the coven. You go get us hot movie stars' autographs."

"And shirtless pictures," Bea added, fanning herself.

"As for the coven, those busybodies will have to come through us first," Helen promised.

Janis sighed. "They're not going to give up easily, you know."

Helen braced her hands on her hips. "We need to buy Riley time until we can come up with a plan to keep her powers under wraps."

Janis leaned forward. "What do you suggest?"

"We call in our favors." Helen's smile promised trouble. "All of them."

Alyce cackled and slapped Janis on the shoulder.

Bea lifted her shot glass in a toast. "To mayhem," she said. "May the best witches win."

Before I left, Helen made me swear I wouldn't tell anyone but our inner circle. Grudgingly, she included my crew and Volkov in that group. Since they'd already witnessed my immunity to magic, we agreed it was better to keep them in the loop than have one of them inadvertently say something damning when the coven started asking questions. And they would most certainly ask questions.

CHAPTER 5

I'd been on plenty of first dates, but none of them started with a helicopter. When Volkov picked me up, he was dressed in form-fitting black clothes that accentuated every muscle in his powerful body. The outfit was a far cry from his usual tailored business suits.

One look at him, and my heart rate kicked up. I'd bit my lip. "Are you about to take me breaking and entering?" I asked breathlessly.

Volkov shook his head with a laugh. "Nothing so dangerous."

I scanned his classic burglar attire with a frown. "Where are you taking me, then?"

He smiled, eyes crinkling at the corners. "It's a surprise."

When we arrived at the downtown airport, my mouth dropped open. Volkov led me straight to a sleek gray Bell helicopter, offering a hand up when I hesitated. Rather than getting in the passenger's side with me, Volkov circled the helicopter and took the pilot's seat.

His phone rang, and he put it on speaker while checking gauges and flipping switches. "What?"

"Sorry to interrupt." Teagan sounded unruffled. As part of the pack's leadership team, Teagan was probably used to his atrocious phone manners. "Daniella called. There's a problem with the charity event venue."

"What kind of problem?"

"Apparently, there was a leak over the summer, and the theater now has black mold growing on the walls. She wanted to know if you'd consider paying for removal."

"Absolutely not." Volkov snapped. "That place needs to be condemned. Call in some favors and get Kauffman Theatre. We can be flexible with the date."

Teagan cleared her throat. "Isn't Kauffman overkill for an event like this?"

"No."

"Alright," she said. "I'll handle it."

"Good. And Teagan, line up a rehearsal space while you're at it."

She sighed. "You got it, boss."

Volkov hung up without saying goodbye.

I raised an eyebrow. "Charity event, huh?"

Volkov shrugged. "It's a tax write-off."

"Right." Because, unlike me, who got paid under the table, Max Volkov ran several successful companies and actually filed his taxes. Like a responsible adult.

I fidgeted with the skirt of the halter dress I'd worn for our first official date. Despite Volkov being dressed more casually than I was for once, I was out of my depth. This dress was the nicest one I owned, and it had cost thirty bucks off the rack. When I'd put it on, I'd assumed that he'd take me to the type of restaurant that gave you more than one fork, as if contaminating dessert with salad was a cardinal sin. In my world, an overpriced meal and an allotment of game tokens at Dave & Busters qualified as a nice date. A destination that required a helicopter was beyond anything I could have prepared for.

It'll be fine, I told myself. *It's just a date. In a helicopter. With a man hot enough to make me forget my Travis Kelce fandom.*

Volkov glanced at my hands that were still twitching on my lap. Worry pinched his brow.

I wanted his easy smile back, so I wiped my clammy palms on my skirt and passed my nervousness off as preflight jitters. "You sure you can fly this thing?"

Volkov relaxed and winked at me, his pale blue eyes stark against his all-black ensemble. "I guess we're about to find out." When he reached for my seatbelt, his familiar scent wrapped around me to settle my nerves while he buckled me in. He handed me a headset that matched his, so we could hear each other during the flight.

It didn't take long to recognize he was more than capable of handling the helicopter. Not that I'd actually doubted it. For the first twenty minutes, I pressed my nose to the glass, excitement at my first helicopter ride distracting me as I took in the view.

When Volkov asked me out, I thought he meant dinner and a movie. I should've known this man wouldn't do anything by half measures. *Did all of his first dates get the helipad treatment?* The thought sat heavy in my mind as I stared out the window.

"Are you planning to tell me where we're going?" I finally asked. It was weird hearing my voice through the headset.

Volkov glanced at me and smiled. "Arkansas."

I wasn't sure what I was expecting, but Arkansas sure wasn't it. "What's in Arkansas?"

"It wouldn't be much of a surprise if I told you." When I started bouncing my leg, Volkov chuckled. "The flight will take a couple hours, so you should settle in. How was magical training?"

Happy to have something to focus on other than the litany of first dates I was imagining him on, I shared Helen's theory. I watched closely for his reaction. At the mention of nulls, he stiffened and clenched his teeth. Even though Volkov would never lay a hand on me in anger, the tight confines of the helicopter suddenly felt stifling. Noting my tension, he took a deep breath before he spoke. "She's sure?"

"Sure enough." I looked out the window again, but this time I couldn't see past my worries. I recounted Helen's prediction about the coven's reaction and her warning not to tell anyone.

"But you told me." Volkov's shoulders eased.

I reached over and squeezed his arm. "You and the team are the exceptions."

He nodded. "Don't trust anyone else with this, Riley, especially Sato."

"Do you think the Enclave would lock me up?" I swallowed past the fear tightening my throat. I'd spent four years under Carl's thumb, my life not my own. No way I could go back to that.

"Look at me," he ordered, a flicker of his wolf in his eyes as they met mine. "No one is going to take your freedom. That I can promise you."

He couldn't. No one could, but I appreciated his conviction, anyway. "Helen and the girls will run interference—buy us some time." I bit the inside of my cheek as I ran through the options. "I can fake being a magical dud as long as the coven doesn't throw spells at me like Helen did. Since I can see wards, I can pretend they stop me like anyone else." It was a long shot. According to Helen, the coven would run the full gamut of magical aptitude tests on me. The chances of them not noticing my immunity to elemental magic was slim. "Or maybe I'll learn to pull a rabbit out of a hat," I joked. "A few botched slight-of-hand tricks, and they'll write me off as not worth their time." Getting people to underestimate me was turning out to be my only superpower.

Volkov frowned. "We'll figure it out."

I forced my worries aside and steered the conversation to lighter things, so we could enjoy the flight. It was mid-afternoon when we arrived in Arkansas. Volkov set the chopper down on a large driveway next to a stunning house at the top of Mount Magazine. At 2,753 feet, Volkov assured me that this was the tallest mountain within date distance. I snickered at that. Date distance didn't typically involve flying.

Although Mount Magazine was considerably smaller than the Rockies, the lush green trees covering it provided a scenic backdrop. Volkov opened my door and gave me a hand down before grabbing a bag from the helicopter and leading me to the entrance. I stared at the timber and stone mountain-top home. There were no signs to indicate it was a lodge or a business. The building was similar enough in style to Volkov's house in Kansas City that I wondered if this could be a second home or investment property.

"Is this yours?" I asked.

"Only for the weekend." He unlocked the front door and waited. "It's a vacation rental."

My eyebrows shot up, and I stared up at him. "You rented a house and a helicopter for our first date?"

"Not quite." He held the door for me. "The helicopter's mine."

I stumbled, spinning to gawk at him.

He nudged me through the door. "I need it for business."

"And for impressing dates," I mumbled.

Volkov grinned. "Is it working?"

"Max, you didn't have to do all this." I looked around the great room as we stepped inside. This was the kind of place you went on vacation, not a first date. "It's too much," I whispered.

"No, it's not," he insisted. Volkov leaned in until only inches separated us. "We only get one first date, Riley. I plan to get it right."

My heart hitched at the sincerity in his expression. A perfect date for me would be paintball or rock climbing or karaoke. Fun and easy. But I didn't say any of that because he did all this for me. It wasn't the cocky alpha I was used to standing in front of me. Right now, he was just a man who wanted to impress a woman with a sincerity that stole my breath.

I nodded because I didn't trust myself to speak.

Volkov's gaze dropped to the pulse hammering in my neck. He bent his head to mine, but instead of kissing me, he brushed his lips against my forehead. I closed my eyes. After a second, he stepped away, breaking the charge that held me to him.

Volkov closed the front door and flipped on the lights while I took in the house. With its exposed timbers and floor-to-ceiling mountain views, the inside was even more stunning than the outside. I crossed the room to the windows.

"The view is gorgeous."

"Yes, it is," Volkov said.

I turned back to him, but he wasn't looking out the

window. His attention was locked on me. Heat bloomed in my chest.

Volkov tossed his bag on the couch and joined me. He wrapped strong arms around me and pulled my back flush against him. I let his heartbeat steady me. Determined to hold on to this, I cataloged everything—the weight of his arms against my ribs, the low hum of the air conditioner cooling my flushed skin, the solid heat of his body behind me, and the endless beauty stretched out before us like a gift. We stood like that for a long time—just the two of us taking in this one perfect moment before our lives crashed back in around us.

The sound of his phone ringing broke the spell.

He answered on the third ring. "Someone better be dying."

Between my shifter senses and our close proximity, I heard Teagan as clearly as if she were speaking to me. "Sorry, boss. Bennie called. A couple of the younger shifters got into a bar brawl at Grinders."

Volkov frowned. "And?"

"The brawl was apparently over a vampire. They're all in lockup. Together."

"Get them out," he said. "Why isn't Ward handling this shit?"

"I called you first, alpha," Teagan said.

"Next time, call him first." Volkov hung up, turned his ringer off, and shoved his phone in his back pocket.

As soon as I settled back in his arms, the doorbell rang. When Volkov ignored it, I tilted my head to gaze up at him. "Shouldn't we get that?"

Whiskey eyes met mine as his wolf peered back at me, and his voice—when it came—was husky. "Stay as you are." He was slow to release me, his knuckles brushing the underside of my breast and making me shiver as he finally let go.

He opened the door to a dark-haired man with a goatee and an armful of groceries. Volkov led the way to the kitchen. Rather than setting the grocery bags on the counter like a delivery person would, the man began putting them in the oversized stainless-steel refrigerator like he lived here. When he finished, he turned to Volkov and extended his hand. "My pleasure to meet you, Mr. Volkov."

Volkov shook his hand before turning to me. "Riley, this is Chef Marco."

"You hired a private chef?" I gaped at them. "For a date?"

Both men smiled indulgently at me as if this were normal.

"He came highly recommended," Volkov assured me.

I stuttered until I found my manners again and moved to shake the man's hand.

"Dinner will be ready at 7:00 as you requested, sir." Chef Marco nodded at us before returning to the kitchen. Since that was still three and a half hours from now, whatever he was cooking probably involved making origami vegetables and fancy sauces to drizzle over perfectly seared Wagyu steaks.

I continued to watch the chef bustle around until Volkov grabbed his bag from the couch. "We should get ready."

"Ready for what?"

"Your surprise." He called over his shoulder as he headed down the hall.

I glanced at the professional chef inventorying the cookware before following Volkov to the master bedroom, my nerves back in full force. I eyed the duffle bag slung over his broad shoulder. If the helicopter and private chef didn't qualify as my surprise, I wasn't sure what to expect. An evening gown rolled up in there? One of those fancy expensive robes high-end spas used for couples' massages?

"What's in the bag?" I asked.

Volkov dropped it on the plaid bedspread and turned to me, humor in his eyes as he took in my wary expression. He reached down and unzipped it, pulling out the contents. To my relief, there were no sequins or silk in sight. With a grin, he handed me utilitarian black hiking pants, a long-sleeved dark jersey, and a pair of black gloves.

I perked up. Maybe we were going to rob a bank after all.

"No felonies," Volkov said, as if reading my mind. He shoved the clothes into my arms, spun me toward the en suite bathroom, and gave me a push. "But I promise you'll like the surprise, anyway."

CHAPTER 6

Once I was dressed, Volkov grabbed my hand and tugged me out the door to a wrap-around deck outfitted with an extravagant kitchen, stone fireplace, and a large hot tub. But the surprise wasn't the mountain-top jacuzzi. It was even better.

Beyond the deck was a dirt path where two top-of-the-line mountain bikes waited for us.

"We're riding down the mountain?" I asked.

"I thought it would be something you'd like to do." He scanned my face to gauge my reaction.

"Are you kidding me?" I grinned. "This is amazing!"

Volkov pulled a helmet off one of the bikes and put it on my head. His, I noticed, didn't come with a helmet.

"Where's yours?" I asked as he fastened it beneath my chin.

He smirked. "I'll be fine."

"If you say so." I grabbed the gloves he'd given me earlier out of my back pocket. "I didn't know you liked to mountain bike."

He shrugged. “I haven’t tried it before.” He handed me a bike and grabbed the other.

My heart did a stupid little flip, knowing he was doing this solely because he thought I’d like it. The last time I’d been on a bike, I’d been eleven years old, cycling through my old neighborhood in Santa Fe with my dad. It was one of the last happy memories I had before everything changed. I glanced at Volkov, who looked far too large on that compact bike, and smiled so wide my cheeks hurt.

Because the beginning of the path was wide enough for two bikes, we rode side-by-side for a few minutes. Although it’d been years since I’d been on one, it didn’t take me long to feel comfortable going faster. Volkov quickly matched my speed, edging past me. Despite it being his first time, he rode with the same confidence he did everything.

“What’s the matter? Afraid I’ll beat you to the bottom?” I teased.

“Hardly,” he scoffed, his competitive streak on full display as he pedaled faster.

I laughed, keeping pace with him. “Do you ever let someone else win?”

Volkov grimaced. “If I let someone win, it wouldn’t actually be a win, now would it?”

I could see the path narrowing up ahead. Whoever got there first would be the first one to the bottom. “In that case, try to keep up.” I bent low over the handlebars and picked up speed.

Despite my frantic pedaling, Volkov beat me to the narrowed section of trail and took the lead. I didn’t see the sharp curve until we were upon it. Although Volkov’s bike skidded, he recovered just in time to avoid wiping out. I narrowly missed a low tree branch as I careened around the bend, but I managed to stay upright, whooping in triumph.

The smart thing to do would have been to slow down.

Neither of us touched the brakes.

We rode the adrenaline rush through several more curves before hitting a bump in the trail that sent us both airborne. Volkov made landing look easy. When it was my turn, the tires hit the ground hard enough to rattle my teeth. At least I kept the bike under me.

Volkov glanced over his shoulder to ensure I was still behind him. That was his first mistake. His second was swerving toward the black bear beside the trail while he was looking at me. The bear stood up straighter and, for one heart-stopping minute, I was certain he'd attack. Volkov roared loud enough it rattled my bones. The bear scrambled away as fast as he could run. While we watched the bear disappear into the trees, Volkov's tire hit a root that sent him crashing into the underbrush face first.

I hit the brakes, laying the bike over in my haste to reach him. I was thankful for the full coverage hiking pants that saved my legs as I slammed into the ground. "Are you okay?" I called from where I lay sprawled and winded.

"I'm fine," he grumbled.

By the time I got to my feet, Volkov was untangling the vine wrapped around his ankle and picking leaves out of his mouth. Beyond a few scrapes and cuts, he appeared uninjured. His bike, however, was a tangled mess, the front wheel bent. There was no way it would be rolling anytime soon. Volkov ran a hand through his dark hair and glared down at the mangled bike.

We sat on a fallen log beside the trail to regroup. I picked a twig off his shirt and nudged his knee with mine. "Not bad for your first time."

Volkov let out a choked laugh. "Does anything get you down?"

I considered it. "Raisins."

He looked at me. "Raisins?"

"You know when you bite into a cookie only to discover that instead of the chocolate chip goodness you deserve, you get a mouthful of freaking raisins?" I shuddered. "That gets me down."

Volkov curled an arm around my waist and pulled me closer. The kiss he gave me started sweet but heated up quickly, that wicked tongue teasing my lips until I let him in. Too soon, he broke the kiss and stood, offering me his hand.

"Since the bikes are trashed, there's only one thing to do." He took off his shirt and dropped it on the mangled bike.

The sight made my mouth go dry. I'd never seen an out-of-shape shifter, but this man was stacked with muscle like a heavyweight fighter. Between that body built for sin and those eyes that flashed from glacial blue to molten amber when he looked at me, Max Volkov outshined even the mountainside view.

My eyes flared wide when he reached for the button on his pants. I forced my gaze away, scanning the trail for signs of the black bear—or worse—other mountain bikers. "You want to have sex here?" I whispered.

Volkov laughed, his shoulders shaking. "I meant we'd shift, Riley." He pointed up the trail the way we came. "We can make it back much faster on four legs than two. I'll send someone back for the bikes."

"Right." I stared at his fingers, still poised on the button of his pants. "We should definitely shift. Good idea." I made no move to shrug out of my own clothes as I ogled him.

Smiling, he took his time unbuttoning his pants and pushing them down his legs, taking his boxers with them. I sucked in a sharp breath. He kept his eyes on me throughout his shift.

Volkov's beast was as breathtaking as the man. Easily double the size of a timber wolf, he was a midnight-black predator with eyes so bright, they held me captive. I admired him before losing my own clothes. Unlike Volkov's instantaneous transformation, mine took several minutes.

Although I was bigger than a standard barnyard goat in this form, I felt small next to the massive werewolf beside me. As a prey animal, I should be wary, but he wasn't a threat to me. Volkov tolerated my affectionate headbutt before nipping my side to prod me into moving. I raced up the mountain with his wolf at my back.

On four legs, the instincts of my goat drove me, but my mind remained my own. Unlike the folk tales, shifters didn't lose themselves when in their animal form. We weren't two separate creatures battling for a body. A shifter had one soul with dual natures and the forms inherent to each. In this skin, I reveled in the freedom to climb a mountain again, my heart lighter by the second.

When we reached the top, we shifted back. Walking inside naked while Chef Marco finished dinner wasn't an option, so I jimmied open the bedroom window to retrieve our clothes before circling around to the front door. Although the chef gave us a measuring look when we strolled in dressed in different clothes than we left wearing, he didn't comment.

The smell of slow-simmered pork and green chiles made my stomach rumble and my eyes tear up. It smelled of home.

Volkov nodded to the chef before giving me his full attention. "With you leaving in the morning, we didn't have time to go to Santa Fe, so I brought a little of New Mexico to you." He rubbed his jaw and watched me.

"This is incredible." I stepped into him, wrapping him in a hug. "Thank you."

We broke apart to freshen up. He took the guest bathroom, and I showered in the master suite. I was sitting on the kitchen counter chatting up the chef when Volkov returned.

"Please," Chef Marco said, gesturing to a table on the deck set with brightly colored Fiesta tableware. "Make yourselves comfortable, and I'll serve the first course."

I turned my head so only Volkov would see me mouth "fancy" at the mention of a first course. In my world, we called those appetizers.

Before I could jump down, Volkov wrapped his hands around my waist and lifted me off the counter. Up close, I noticed the flush that started under the collar of his shirt and colored his cheeks. His fingers lingered on my hips, and I waited for him to kiss me again.

Chef Marco cleared his throat. We broke apart and headed for the deck.

Volkov held my chair before taking his seat, ignoring the phone now buzzing in his back pocket.

"Pack business?" I asked.

"It's not important."

My first bite of bacon-wrapped chile rellenos cemented Chef Marco's reputation. The green chile stew and artisan bread he brought next qualified as full-on food porn. By the time he set the sopapillas in front of us, I was professing my undying love. Chef Marco beamed at me and thanked Volkov before seeing himself out.

Volkov watched me savor the last of my meal and ran a hand across his flushed face.

"Too spicy?" I asked. Volkov didn't share my chile pepper appreciation, but he ate everything Chef Marco made us without complaint. I'd lived in Kansas so long that even my lips tingled from the heat.

"No. It's great," Volkov said, pulling his shirt away from his body as if he needed to cool off. "From the moaning, I'm guessing the food lived up to your standards?" he teased.

"Everything was amazing, Max."

I licked a drizzle of honey off the corner of my mouth. He leaned across the table, watching me intently.

"Riley?"

With Chef Marco gone, we were alone. "Yes?" It came out breathier than I'd intended.

"What's wrong with your lips?"

"My lips?" I ran my thumb across my lower lip, noticing the swelling. I frowned and looked closer at the flush on Volkov's skin. "Your face." I shot to my feet and rounded the table for a better look. "How many leaves were there?"

"What?"

"When you fell off your bike, how many leaves were on those stems you picked out of your mouth?" I prompted. "Leaves of three, let it be."

He groaned. "Poison ivy." Volkov scratched the side of his neck and then cursed under his breath. "The kiss. I spread it to your lips."

"It's not your fault."

His jaw clenched. "It is."

I reached for him, but he scrambled away so fast, his chair crashed to the deck.

"You shouldn't touch me." He scratched his cheek, the

angry red rash more noticeable by the second. He held a hand up when I stepped closer. "I don't want to make it worse."

"We've both showered, so it's no longer on our skin," I reasoned. "It'll be gone in a few hours, a day at most." As shifters, accelerated healing ensured that a rash like this would clear up far faster than if we were human. "Let's enjoy our night."

Volkov stiffened. "I wanted to give you the perfect date." He stared at my mouth. "Not an allergic reaction."

I resisted the urge to rub my lips to stop the tingling. Scratching wouldn't help, and he felt bad enough without drawing more attention to it. I grabbed his hands before he could pull away and met his eyes. "You did."

He barked out a laugh. "Not even you could spin this disaster into a perfect date, Riley."

I squeezed his hands. "You listen to me, Max Volkov." I looked at the remnants of our meal and at the mountain path visible from where we stood on the deck. "No one has ever put this much effort in for me." My voice faltered. I'd never been the type of woman men pulled out all the stops to impress. Before I met this man, I'd never wanted to be.

Volkov reeled me in, holding me tight against his body. "Well, get used to it," he rumbled.

I swallowed the emotion. "Besides," I said, pulling back to look up at him. "Helen will die laughing when I tell her you face-planted into a patch of poison ivy because you were scared I'd beat you down the mountain."

As I'd hoped, his stormy expression eased. "Beat me? I was definitely winning."

"Of course, you were." I tapped the angry red rash spreading across his stubbled cheek. "So much winning."

He squeezed me tighter.

When his phone vibrated, I snagged it out of his back pocket and handed it to him. "You might as well answer it. Teagan will keep calling." From the incessant phone calls, being alpha meant fielding more dumpster fires than I'd imagined. And here I assumed it was all about bossing people around.

"It's not like this date could get any worse," Volkov grumbled as he took the phone out of my hand and put it on speaker to answer it. "What is it now, Teagan?"

"Sorry to bother you again, alpha, but you have an unexpected visitor."

"I won't get back until late, and I'm in no mood to entertain guests." He closed his eyes briefly and pinched the bridge of his nose. Then he scratched it. "Get rid of them."

Teagan coughed. "I don't think that's going to work."

He sighed. "Why is that?"

"Because it's your mother."

CHAPTER 7

We were all settled in the chartered plane's cushy seats on the way to Los Angeles before anyone gave me grief about my date night memento.

"How much did the two of you kiss last night?" Kali asked. "Your lips are so puffy it looks like you got filler injected."

Dez leaned closer to get a better look and winced. "Maybe invest in some lip balm. That looks painful."

Nash and Ward kept their comments to themselves, but both men couldn't stop staring at my mouth.

"If you think this is bad, you should've seen me last night." I smacked my lips and immediately regretted it. The swelling had gone down enough I was now rocking bee-stung lips rather than the punched-in-the-mouth look from yesterday. I spent the next ten minutes recounting our little mountain biking adventure.

Even Ward was chuckling. "I wish I would've seen Max's face," he said. "Irina will have a field day with this."

"Irina who?" Dez asked me.

Craig answered. "Irina Volkov, Max's mother. She showed

up unannounced yesterday while he and Riley were chasing bears."

"We weren't chasing the bear." I laughed.

Kali rubbed her hands together. "I'd pay good money to watch that man have a pissing contest with a black bear."

"Please." I rolled my eyes. "That poor bear wouldn't stand a chance."

"The poison ivy on the other hand—" Nash said. "Noxious weed: 1. Alpha werewolf: 0."

I smiled at the good-natured ribbing. All of this—the easy camaraderie, the first-class travel, the anticipation of a good heist—was what I imagined when I pulled this team together. Not even swollen lips could dim my smile.

Kali drummed her fingernails on her slate gray cigarette pants, her version of casual clothes, and studied me. "You really like him, don't you?"

My smile widened. "I do."

Kali and Volkov rarely saw eye-to-eye, but my admission changed things. Oh, she'd still give him grief, but the understanding that passed between us now meant she knew he and I were way past casual hookups. As scary as the prospect was, I might be playing for keeps.

Kali dipped her head in acknowledgement. "But you're not at the meet-his-mother stage yet?"

I glanced down at my broken-in combat boots and ripped jeans. The idea of meeting Max's mother sent me into panic mode, but I made light of the question. "Like this?" I pointed to my lips and made a duck face. "Not the first impression I hope to make."

Thankfully, I was on a flight to Hollywood, which granted me a reprieve, and I was going to make the most of it. With any luck, Irina Volkov would be gone long before I got back to Kansas City.

Nash pointed at the stack of manilla folders Dez brought on board and changed the subject. "Those for us?"

"They are." Dez sorted through the folders and distributed them, keeping the fattest one for himself. "Inside you'll find your cover identities and resumés. I altered as little as possible, so you'd have less to remember." He looked pointedly at Nash.

Nash took his folder. "Good call. Keep it simple."

Dez frowned at the rare bit of praise. "You must be tired," he muttered.

He wasn't wrong. When Nash handed Garth off to Helen for rooster-sitting duty this morning, he'd complained about Garth waking him at all hours of the night by standing on his chest and crowing in his face.

Despite the lack of sleep, Garth was good for him. His antics meant less time for Nash to wallow in the past. *They'd bond eventually.*

After flipping through my folder, I whistled. "Wow, Dez. You made me a badass."

He grinned. "Since you'll be doing stunts, I got creative."

I ticked off my newfound skills. "Proficient in two martial arts—" I fist pumped. "Trained in acrobatics, former gymnast, and an avid rock climber and skydiver." The mention of gymnastics reminded me of my mother. I ignored the pang in my chest and nudged Nash with my toe. "You hear that, Nash? I'm basically Special Forces."

Nash snorted. "Last I checked, the Green Berets didn't require many cartwheels."

I tsked. "With the motto 'be prepared,' maybe they should."

"Pretty sure that's the Boy Scouts," Nash corrected.

Close enough. I scanned my fake resumé. "I'm also a card-carrying member of a stunt guild—whatever that is."

"It's the CYA the studio needs for insurance," Dez said.

"Sweet." Unlike most resumés, this one included my head-shot and measurements. My height wasn't a great secret, but I was impressed that Dez noted my weight accurately. "I can't believe you guessed how much I weigh."

"I didn't." Dez pushed his glasses up his nose. "I hacked into your medical records."

We all stared at him.

"What?" he snapped.

Nash shook his head. "Wouldn't it have been easier just to ask?"

Dez shrugged. "Not really."

Before they could devolve into a bickering match, I turned to Kali. "What skills did he give you?"

She stuck a sheet of paper under my nose. "I'll have you know this is my actual resumé."

"Because she had the prerequisite costuming experience, there was no need to embellish hers," Dez said.

Like Kali's, Nash's bio stuck pretty close to his actual background. Apparently, stamping ex-Green Beret on an application was enough to land a security job.

We spent the remainder of the flight memorizing our potential marks. Dez's deep dive into the cast and crew provided us with a twelve-page dossier, complete with glossy, full-color photographs. Although we wouldn't be working directly with Monty Corville, daredevil extraordinaire and possible blood sucker, we would be working alongside a cast of B movie veterans. They included a guy who played in my favorite campy werewolf flick and a former Miss Nevada who we recognized from her cameo in a prescription ad campaign for irritable bowel syndrome.

Kali tossed her cast list on her seat and stood to grab a couple bottles of chilled water from the fancy little fridge onboard. "I take it we won't be working on a summer blockbuster."

"Hardly," Dez said.

"Good. It'll be easier to infiltrate a mid-budget movie set." Craig glanced at Kali. "Safer, too."

Kali chuckled and handed him a bottle of water before sitting beside him. "Infiltrate? Really?"

Nash grunted his agreement.

"The only thing I want to infiltrate is the costume stash," Kali said. "What's the name of this movie, anyway?"

Dez ran his fingers through his messy red hair, looking sheepish. "I don't know. *Dive* or *Jump*—some action word."

Everyone looked at each other and shrugged. It's not like we'd be on set long enough to make the credits. But between the potential names and the skydiving experience Dez listed for me, it sounded like we'd definitely be working on an action flick.

"I might get to jump out of a plane," I mused. One more thing to check off my bucket list.

Dez patted my knee. "You do realize you're new to doing stunts, right? You probably won't actually be jumping out of a plane."

That sucked. I snatched a glossy photo of an actor in a bad werewolf costume and clutched it to my chest. "At least I can get the big bad wolf's autograph as a consolation prize."

Craig sighed. "I thought now that you were dating, you'd stop antagonizing Max. I'm the one who has to deal with his cranky ass, you know."

I widened my eyes. "I have no idea what you're talking about. I'm merely collecting valuable Hollywood memorabilia here." I'd totally be framing this baby to give to Max for Christmas.

Nash grunted and pulled his baseball cap lower over his eyes, so he could nap. I took pity on him and dimmed the interior lights for the remainder of the flight.

When we landed, our first order of business after picking up the rental van was to drive by Monty Corville's posh Studio City home. Although we'd need to verify whether Corville was supernatural or not and determine if he was working alone, there was no time like the present to case his house. As our designated driver, Craig parked down the block from Corville's place.

Corville lived in a sleek, white two-story home with a maple front door and modern black accents. Except for Dez's apartment, the only vampire residences I'd been in were those I'd broken into, so I wasn't exactly an expert on vamp real estate. Still, from the number of shadeless windows on Corville's home, all signs pointed to him being human. While vampires could walk in the sun like humans, their eyes were sensitive, and they preferred the dark.

The neighborhood itself was upscale without being over-the-top pretentious, with ample trees and cars lining both sides of the street. In Kansas, this would be a nice upper-middle class neighborhood. But we weren't in Kansas. "How much would a place like this set you back?" I asked.

"More than I make in a year," Kali said.

Dez stared at his phone when he answered. "$3.5 million. According to Zillow, that's what Corville paid for the place when he bought it six months ago."

I whistled. "Looks like stunt work pays better than burglary."

Dez looked up from his phone. "That or he has another source of income."

As I'd learned with Dez, plenty of vampires had nest eggs built before they were turned. The fact that Corville possessed a rare demon artifact indicated he had a fat bank account, regardless of how he acquired it.

I scanned the house, noting the security sign in the front yard and the various access points. "We need a better look at the back of his house."

"That's why I brought this." Dez dug out the mini drone he brought and turned it on.

"You don't think he's going to spot that thing buzzing around his yard?" Nash asked.

Dez huffed. "Not when I'm done, no." He pulled out the iridescent illusion potion Janis mixed for him and doused the drone with it.

"Woah!" Kali pivoted in the front seat for a better look. "I can't see it at all." She waved her hands around until she bumped the drone.

"That's what an invisibility potion does," Dez said dryly, shooting Nash a smug smile. "It's sound-dampening as well."

I couldn't see the drone, but I could make out the residual magic covering it. "How will you fly it if you can't see it?" I asked Dez, keeping my hands in my lap. Unlike Kali, I couldn't risk nullifying the spell by touching the drone.

Rather than getting out of the van to launch it, which would draw attention to us, Dez rolled down his window. "I'll navigate using this." He held up a remote with a small screen on it and launched the drone. "It has built-in anti-crash technology, so it'll sense and avoid bumping into objects." He pointed at the remote. "And if I push this return-to-home button, the drone will come back to its launch location."

Nash's expression was bored, but he leaned closer to see the camera footage. *Boys and their toys.*

Once Dez captured the surveillance footage we needed to plan the heist, we drove to the rental house to drop our luggage before exploring the area. After taking the requisite photos of the Hollywood sign and stopping for sushi—my idea—Kali persuaded us to check out the walk of fame. When we spotted Kalien L. Clive's Hollywood star, she stood on top of every letter but those in her name. With her stylish clothes, oversized sunglasses, and silk scarf holding back her long dark hair, Kali looked every bit a glamorous movie star. I snapped a photo on her cellphone. Then I sent myself a copy, so I'd have more than faux lip filler as a souvenir.

CHAPTER 8

Next time, Dez wouldn't be the one choosing our accommodations. Sharing one full bathroom with four other people meant I'd be leaving the house with my hair still wet from my five-minute shower. I threw it into a high ponytail that dripped down the back of my shirt while I ate my second bowl of cereal. I'd need the fuel for the high-octane stunts I'd be performing today.

I checked my phone. Three missed calls and a voicemail from a number I didn't recognize. I listened to the voicemail, which was an invitation to come by the Kansas City coven headquarters for a friendly meet and greet. Despite Martha's chirpy little invite, all I heard was the thinly veiled threat to my freedom. I deleted the voicemail and put my phone on silent.

Kali strolled into the kitchen, somehow looking put together despite the limited bathroom time. "You excited?" she asked.

"Hell yeah." I offered her the cereal box. "I wonder if I'll get to swing on one of those wires like a superhero."

Kali bypassed the cereal for the coffee. "Probably." She took a big gulp before screwing the lid on her travel mug. "I can't wait to pick up insider costuming tips from pros." She glanced down at the high-waisted black shorts and off-the-shoulder polka dot top she wore with a frown. "Do you think this is okay?"

I raised a brow. "Are you asking me for fashion advice?"

She eyed my plain jeans and gray t-shirt and laughed. "I retract that question." She grabbed a bowl and the box of cereal and sat beside me.

Craig snatched the sugary cereal out of her hands. "Don't eat that crap. I'll make you an omelet."

She wrapped her arms around his waist and squeezed. "I'm keeping you."

He dropped a kiss on her head before rummaging in the fridge for the groceries we'd picked up last night. He pulled out a carton of eggs. "Anyone else?" When I raised my hand, Craig's lips quirked as he eyed my cereal. "Are you ever not hungry?"

I shrugged.

Craig turned to Dez and Nash who'd just joined us. "What about you two?"

They stopped sniping at each other long enough to say yes. Now that everyone was here, it was time to finalize our game plan.

I looked between Craig and Dez. "Which one of you is dropping us off?"

"I will," Craig said. "Today, I'll scout Corville's neighborhood and watch his place to make sure no one else tries to take that spell book."

One less thing to worry about. With Craig on guard duty, no one would get past him.

"What about you, Dez?" I asked.

"While you're all living the glamorous life, I'll dig up what I can online about Corville's place. I should be able to find the layout and some interior photos from the last time the house was on the market. I'll also check out the drone footage I took last night."

"Great," I said. We'd need to plot the best way in and out. "Can you also check to see if that security sign in his front yard was for display or if it's actually monitored?" There were a surprising number of homes with security company logos in their windows that were little more than bumper stickers since owners were notorious for letting the contracts lapse. Even if it was active, it'd be standard suburban security—easy to bypass.

"On it." Dez poured himself a glass of orange juice and added a splash of the chilled blood he'd brought. He grimaced but downed the concoction without gagging, which was progress. "I'll also dig deeper into Corville's background, see what he was doing six months ago before he turned up on the stunt scene and let you know if anything interesting turns up."

"That's a good idea." I looked at Nash. "As part of the security staff, you can keep eyes on Corville. I'll do my best to bump into him on set, but I won't be able to watch to see who he talks to or where he goes."

Nash dug into the omelet Craig handed him. "I'll find out if anyone suspicious has turned up since the artifact made the rounds on entertainment tv."

Craig passed out the remaining plates. "And you'll watch for threats and keep these two safe." Although Craig's words were directed at Nash, his attention was on Kali.

"That goes without saying, man," Nash said.

Kali smiled at us over the top of her coffee mug. "I'm on

gossip duty. By the end of the day, I'll have more intel than the lot of you," she promised. Knowing Kali, she probably would.

My phone screen lit with an incoming video call from Helen. Had I not been checking the time, I would have missed it with my ringer off. I accepted the call. When it connected, Helen pointed her camera at Garth, who fluffed his feathers and stared into the lens.

"Hello there, pretty boy," I crooned, pushing my empty plate away. "Are you having a good time?"

Helen turned the camera, so I could see her. They were in the back room of the Stitch Witch. Helen glanced at Garth, who was now wandering around the outside of the playpen she'd set up, attacking the netting. "The poor little guy must've been exhausted. He slept well past dawn without a peep."

Nash coughed, hitting his chest with a fist to dislodge the bite of eggs he'd swallowed. "Are you shitting me? He slept through the night for you."

"Oh yes." Helen peered at Garth. "But he's agitated this morning." She lowered her voice. "He thinks you abandoned him."

Nash scoffed. "I suppose the rooster told you that."

Helen bristled. "As a matter of fact, he did."

"Let me guess," Nash said. "He crowed."

Helen jabbed a bony finger at the camera. "You better watch your tone, sonny." When Nash held his hands up in defeat, she shot him another warning look but stopped pointing at him. "When Janis did her morning tarot spread, the little guy kept pecking at the death card."

Nash looked at the ceiling and took a deep breath. "He's a rooster, Helen. He pecks things."

"He didn't peck any of the other cards—only the death

card," she countered. "He's obviously worried you've abandoned him. You need to reassure him that you're coming home." She turned the camera toward Garth, who stopped circling the playpen and waited expectantly, his beady red eyes practically glowing.

When Nash kept staring at the light fixture on the ceiling, I kicked him under the table.

"Fine," he growled, looking at the video. "I'll be home in a few days. Hang out with the nice witches and be a good chicken."

Dez snickered. I kicked him, too.

"That's better." Helen beamed, hand feeding Garth a freeze-dried black fly larvae from the chicken treats she'd ordered off the internet. She put a little pile on the floor to keep him occupied. "Now then, are you ready for your big debut, hon?"

I grinned. "I'm about to be living my best life out here. I might even get to jump out of a plane."

Dez rolled his eyes and took another bite of his omelet.

"That sounds fun," Helen said. "If my knees were a little younger, I'd like to try it."

I smiled. "What about you? Is the coven harassing you?" I'd hoped with me out of town, they'd leave the girls alone, but after the voicemail Martha left, I doubted it.

Bea cackled in the background. "Oh, don't you worry, sugar. We're keeping them plenty distracted."

"What does that mean?" I asked.

Helen's eyes twinkled as she leaned closer. "That means Operation Cicada is underway."

"Operation Cicada?" Craig asked with a frown. "Like the bug?"

"One hundred to be exact." Helen rubbed her hands together. "You remember Stan the Exterminator?"

I shook my head. "Not really."

She huffed. "Well, he owed me a favor, and I called it in."

Janis leaned into the frame. "Helen made him release a hundred live cicadas into coven headquarters, and then she called an anonymous tip into the health department."

Helen grinned. "That little juice bar of theirs is subject to health inspections."

I laughed. That was one way to keep the coven busy.

"Remind me not to cross you ladies," Craig said with a straight face.

After giving us the blow-by-blow of Operation Cicada and making me promise to take lots of pictures, we said our good-byes. An hour later, Craig dropped us in the studio parking lot. We split up, ready for our first day rubbing elbows with the Hollywood elite.

CHAPTER 9

The pleated skirt Kali tossed hit me dead center in the chest. I held it away from my body with a curled lip. "What is this?"

"Your costume." Kali rooted around until she came up with ugly bloomers, a fitted top with a giant B on it, and an honest-to-God hair bow.

It turned out that *Jump* wasn't a high-octane skydiving flick after all.

"I'm not wearing that." I tried to hand everything back, but Kali shoved the outfit into my hands.

"You'll look cute," she assured me. "Until you're covered in blood, anyway."

At least when we got to the bloody bits of this cheerleader slasher movie, it might be fun. Because this was for the greater good—and, more importantly—because I didn't have a choice if I wanted to get paid, I changed into the ugly 1980s cheerleader costume.

So far, nothing about this day was living up to my expectations. After spending an hour filling out boring paperwork and watching HR videos, the clipboard toting drill sergeant in a pencil skirt who I reported to this morning introduced me to Trevor, the stunt coordinator. Trevor had taken one look at me, jerked his head toward the costume trailer, and told me I had thirty minutes.

I stared into the full-length mirror while Kali fitted me with a brunette wig, fastening the hideous blue hair bow to my ponytail. Kali snapped a picture before I knew what she was doing.

"Hey!" I scrambled for her phone, but she stuck it in her back pocket, so I couldn't delete the photographic evidence. "You're enjoying this far too much," I grumbled.

"That skirt isn't even the best part." She twirled her finger in a circle. "Do a little spin for me, so I can check out your bloomers."

I flipped up the skirt and looked over my shoulder at the outline of an eagle on my backside. "Why would they do this?"

She smirked. "It's your mascot."

"Because nothing says school spirit like an eagle on your left ass cheek." I let the skirt drop.

Before I could stop her, Kali lifted my skirt and snapped another photo. "For the scrapbook."

"Great." I checked my watch. Fifteen minutes before I needed to report on set. All joking aside, I pulled Kali into the costume racks where we had a semblance of privacy and lowered my voice. "Discover any good dirt yet?"

She peered around me to make sure no one was listening. "Rumor has it that Monty Corville has slept his way through half the crew. And according to Stella—the makeup assistant—he has quite the interesting collection of piercings, if you know what I mean."

"Not quite the intel I was after."

Kali pursed her lips until I mimed zipping mine. "We're also not the only ones who've been asking questions about him. Stella said about a week ago, a man posing as a detective showed up right after Corville left for the day asking about the crew. He claimed he was investigating a theft, but he seemed particularly interested in Corville."

I frowned. "How'd she know he wasn't a real detective?"

Kali leveled me with an are-you-kidding look. "Hello. We create illusions for a living."

"Fair enough," I conceded. "Did she say what kinds of questions the guy asked?"

"Where Corville lived. Who he associated with. That kind of thing." Kali lowered her voice. "And earlier this morning, Stella's girlfriend, who works on the movie Corville's in, saw a woman who appeared to be late-forties hanging around Corville's sound stage before she snuck into his dressing room."

"He has a dressing room?" I didn't even get a locker. And Kali confiscated my fanny pack and insisted I carry a purse, which was seriously cramping my style. I'd probably forget the dumb thing somewhere.

"Not the point," Kali said.

"Did she say what this woman looked like?" I asked. Given Corville's free love attitude, chances were the woman was a hookup. But it was a lead worth checking out.

Kali shook her head. "Stella said the woman wore a red scarf around her hair and tortoise shell sunglasses like she didn't want to be identified. All Stella could tell me was that the woman was blonde."

An image of Zara Bellarose's long blonde hair immediately came to mind. Could she be after our artifact? The Enclave released her last week, so it was a stretch that she'd be in California already chasing our mark. Yet, I couldn't rule it out either. From the kill order Sato put on the table, this demon book of spells was even more dangerous than the Cuffs of Valac she'd stolen. She had a history of going after dangerous spells, like the blood-tracing spell Isaac pulled from Kali's memory.

"Did you tell Nash?"

"Yeah." Kali tapped her phone. "Didn't you see the group text?"

Although everyone bitched about it, I'd set up the heist crew group chat to make sharing info like this easier. "Sorry. I turned my ringer off." I checked my phone. Sure enough, there was a string of missed texts, including the photos Kali took of me wearing this ridiculous cheerleading costume—bloomers and all. "Really?"

She grinned, unrepentant. "Nash will be watching for the blonde."

If it was Zara Bellarose, Nash would recognize her since he'd gotten a good look at her before we turned her over to Sato's custody. "Good. Listen, I gotta run."

"Put a little pep in your step," she called after me. "You're in uniform."

I flipped her the bird.

An hour later, the harried stunt coordinator barked out directions in what might as well have been a foreign language. I leaned closer to the perky cheer captain standing next to me. "What's a basket toss?"

She gasped. "You're kidding, right?"

Trevor the stunt coordinator snapped his fingers at me. "Alright new girl, you're our flyer. We'll keep it basic today, so new girl has time to learn the full choreography."

I gave him two thumbs up. Flying sounded a lot more

appealing than cheer routines. Maybe I'd get to swan around on a wire after all.

"Ryan and Seth are bases." Trevor pointed to two stocky men who looked like they lived for the weight machines. "Kelsey, you spot." When I stood waiting for further instructions, Trevor snapped his fingers again. "Time is money. Let's go!"

I took the position in the middle where Trevor pointed. Ryan and Seth faced each other and locked wrists. When I didn't immediately do whatever it was they were waiting for, Trevor stalked over. "You do have cheer experience, right?"

"Yeah." I cheered on the girls plenty during paintball wars. *That counted, right?* "I'm a bit rusty, that's all."

With a long-suffering sigh, Trevor went through the basket toss step-by-step. Because the other three seemed to be doing all the work in this scenario, I was happy to let them pitch me in the air. It was more fun than I expected—at least until I caught sight of Trevor's expression as he stomped back over.

"What was that?" he demanded. He mimicked flailing arms and the weird faces I must have made mid-toss.

"Sorry." After three more tries, I had to come clean about my lack of cheer experience. No one seemed surprised. "I'm a fast learner though. I'll have it by tomorrow." Tonight, I'd be doing my homework. If I could learn how to make a functional Molotov cocktail from an online video, surely, I could master cheer stunts. "I'm much better at fight scenes," I assured Trevor, knowing that this afternoon we were filming a scene of me fending off an attacker.

Trevor gritted his teeth. "Fine. But you better have it down by tomorrow."

I nodded enthusiastically and slunk off to find Kali for lunch.

"Come on," she laughed a few minutes later, handing me half a turkey sandwich. "It couldn't have been that bad."

"It was that bad," I said around a mouthful of bread.

We compared notes, but so far, neither of us had seen Corville.

"We're filming the fight scene on a different sound stage, so hopefully I can bump into him this afternoon," I said. "Did you hear any more about the woman spotted going into his dressing room this morning?"

Kali shook her head. "No. Nash said he couldn't find a trace of her on the camera footage. It could be nothing."

Or it could be Zara Bellarose trying to beat me to my prize. I polished off the last of the sandwich and stood. "I'm going to snoop around."

As luck would have it, Monty Corville was working at the sound stage next to the one where I was filming. I fangirl'd over him as an excuse to get close, but even face-to-face, it was hard to tell whether Corville was human or supernatural. With his surfer hair, hard body, and easy smile, he was exceptionally attractive, like vampires tended to be. However, pretty men seemed to be the norm around here.

One thing was certain, the man had enough charisma to draw a crowd. I wasn't the only one clamoring for his attention. While Corville autographed a random receipt I pickpocketed on the walk over, I scanned the area for the woman who had been hanging around this morning. There were plenty of blondes milling around, but none of them were hiding behind tortoise shell sunglasses and red scarves. Before I could draw Corville into a conversation, Trevor showed up and herded me back to work.

Unlike the cheer routine, the fight choreography was easy to pick up. Trevor demoed with the male stuntman I'd be fighting off in a classic locker scene. My attacker would grab me from behind. I'd struggle and then elbow him to break free. Once he released me, I'd run through the showers where I was supposed to slip on the wet floor. At that point, I'd be done, and the camera would cut to the actress looking up at her attacker.

The hardest part would be getting the fall right. While my stunt partner wore pads under his clothes, my cheer costume didn't allow for them. The only thing between me and the slick shower floor was a cheap skirt and good reflexes. Luckily, I wasn't human. Even if I cracked my head on the tile floor, I'd be fine. I walked through my part twice in slow-mo.

Satisfied, Trevor motioned for the camera operators, who crowded into the already confined space of the locker room. Being the center of attention kicked my nerves into high gear, a rush of adrenaline normally reserved for heists flooding my body. I tried to tune everyone out, so I could nail my part and get into Trevor's good graces.

The attack went exactly as we'd practiced—right up until the distinct snap of a rib cracking beneath the impact of my well-placed elbow. My stunt partner swore and put some distance between us.

I spun around to survey the damage with a wince. "Are you okay?"

He hissed in a breath and took another step away from me. "You broke my rib."

"Sorry." I scanned his torso, spotting the faint outline of the pad over his middle. "I thought the padding would protect you."

He glared at me. "Not from a blow like that. You're supposed to pull your punches."

It was an elbow, not a punch, but this didn't seem like a good time to correct him. "Sorry," I muttered again.

While my stunt partner hobbled off to have his rib checked, Trevor pointed a finger in my face. "You're fired."

When I attempted to reason with him, he threatened to have security toss me out.

"I'm going." I walked past the camera operators who were now giving me a wide berth as if their ribs were at risk.

Thankfully, Trevor didn't escort me off set, so I had time to duck behind a sound stage and make an emergency phone call. "Hey Dez. I'm gonna need a favor." I peered around the corner to make sure Trevor hadn't followed me. "How do you feel about compelling the stunt coordinator into giving me my job back?"

CHAPTER 10

"First day went that well, huh?" Nash dropped into the lounge chair next to me and handed me a bowl of mint chocolate chip ice cream drowning in hot fudge.

I snorted but took the ice cream, spooning a bite into my mouth. "I thought I'd be a natural."

Nash's lips twitched. "I saw the footage. You looked like a natural fighter, kicking that guy's ass."

I groaned. "He was wearing padding. How was I supposed to know he couldn't take a hit?" I shoveled another spoonful of ice cream into my mouth and stared at the Hollywood hills from the deck of our rental. Dez might have skimped on the bathrooms, but he got this view right.

Nash nudged my leg, his hazel eyes dancing with humor. "What an absolute wimp."

"Right?" I offered him a bite, but he waved it off. "Maybe I should stick to the one thing I am a natural at—stealing shit." Stunt work was right up there with magic on the list of things I was not good at.

Nash studied me. "Did I ever tell you about my first week in basic training?"

"No."

Nash never talked about his time in the Army. But even with the scruffy beard and rumpled clothes, Nash Mitchell still carried himself like a soldier. They'd cut him loose as easy as Trevor had fired me today despite the years he'd served as a Green Beret. Like me, Nash couldn't be compelled. That made him as uncontrollable as my newly discovered null powers made me. They'd gone to great lengths to tarnish his name, to paint him as an unhinged conspiracy theorist—all because he wouldn't look the other way when he saw the demons that walked among us.

Nash leaned back on the lounger. "The day I turned eighteen, I walked into an Army recruiting office and enlisted. A few weeks later, I was on a bus bound for South Carolina for basic training. All I took with me was a change of clothes, some toiletries, and an old, dog-eared country music magazine." He looked over to make sure I was listening. "Back then, I was another scrawny kid who dreamed of playing at the Grand Ole Opry." Since he went by Nash instead of Wade, the country music aspirations weren't a shocker.

"Why join the Army then?" I asked. "Why not get on a bus for Nashville?"

He took the spoon from my hand and ate a bite of ice cream before handing it back to me. "Because I was dirt poor growing up. Dreams don't pay the bills."

Didn't I know it? I set the bowl aside and leaned back on my lounger. "How was basic training?"

Nash laughed. "Terrible. But then, it's supposed to be." He caught my eye. "Like you, I was cocky enough to think I'd be a natural."

I grinned. "And I take it, you weren't?"

Nash shook his head ruefully. "No. I was not, but I made it through." He looked out at the fading sunset before continuing his story. "That first week was an absolute shit show. First, they shaved off my mullet."

I snort laughed. "Tell me you did not actually have a mullet."

Nash didn't confirm or deny it. "And then they handed me my uniform and pointed me to a bunk in a room full of other cocky eighteen-year-olds." He looked at me. "Do you have any idea what a room like that smells like? Not good, Cruz. Not good. That wasn't even the worst part. Our drill sergeant was a mean S.O.B. named Maddoc Cole. He called himself Mad Dog."

I rolled my eyes.

Nash tucked a hand beneath his head and stared up at the sky. "I had the misfortune of running into Sergeant Cole right off the bus before I knew who he was. When I saw his last name on his uniform and those sparkling green eyes of his, I did the one thing you should never do in basic training—draw attention to myself. I asked if he was related to Lana Cole before I thought better of it."

"The country singer?"

"The country singer." Nash sighed. "Turned out, Lana Cole was his mother, but he didn't appreciate the question. He took great pleasure in busting my balls after that."

"Let me guess, the moral is you got off to a rocky start but persevered." I saluted him.

Nash shook his head. "Oh, that's not the story. The disaster started with the first barracks' inspection. Every day, they checked to make sure you made your bed according to regulation, that you shined your boots, and generally jumped through their endless hoops. When we got word Sergeant Cole was headed over to do that first inspection, I panicked. That dog-eared country magazine I brought—Lana Cole was on the cover."

My eyes widened, and I clapped a hand over my mouth imagining Nash's panic.

"I knew I needed to get rid of that magazine before he saw it. The rest of the guys were rushing around dusting and straightening their sheets, while I was searching for the magazine to hide it. I looked everywhere, even dumped out my bag. I couldn't find it. When I sat on the bed to look under it, I was so distracted I sat on an open bottle of sunscreen. It went everywhere—on the blanket, all over my pants. It even squirted on the floor."

I cringed, imagining the mess. "What did you do?"

"I grabbed a box of tissues and cleaned it up as best I could. Of course, Sergeant Cole showed up before I finished. He marched straight over to my bunk, turned six shades of red from screaming in my face, and tore off all the bedding." Nash choked back a laugh. "And that's when I remembered where I put the magazine. Under my pillow. Open to the full-page spread of Lana Cole decked out in a red, white, and blue bikini." He turned his head and caught my eyes. "And there I was, surrounded by wadded up tissues full of white sunscreen and a half-naked photo of his mother."

I laughed so hard I got a stitch in my side and tears in my eyes. When I could finally catch my breath again, I looked at Nash. "You made that up. There's no way that story's real."

Nash shrugged. "Point is your first day on set—it could've been a helluva lot worse." He stood, offering me a hand up. "Now quit sulking, and let's get to work."

Everyone else was in the living room waiting for us. We

spent the next hour recounting what we'd learned on set. Nash was right. The day wasn't a total loss. Thanks to Dez's intervention, I still had a job. And because I incapacitated my stunt partner, Monty Corville was filling in for him tomorrow, which would give me the chance to determine whether he was human or supernatural.

Although Nash checked the security footage, he didn't find any sign of the detective Stella told Kali about. "Either he was really lucky, or he knew how to avoid the cameras," Nash said.

"And the woman?"

Dez flipped his laptop around and tapped the screen. "We think this is her." The footage showed a woman matching the description. With her scarf and sunglasses, the picture didn't do us much good since her features were obscured. Dez zoomed in, and I looked for any identifying details.

"There." I pointed to her wrist. "Can you enlarge it?"

The close-up was blurry, but I could make out the quartz bracelet the woman wore on her wrist. Plenty of people other than witches wore crystal jewelry these days, but the sight of it made me uneasy. It was chunky enough to cover a thorn and rose vine tattoo. "Do you think that's Bellarose?" I voiced the fear I'd been carting around all day.

My fear wasn't only about her beating me to that demon spell book either. I had no idea why Zara Bellarose unlocked my magic, but I didn't believe for a second it was out of the goodness of her heart. She had an agenda, and until I figured out what it was, I didn't want to be anywhere near her.

Craig leaned closer to the screen. "It's hard to tell. This woman looks shorter than Bellarose, but I can't say for sure."

"Since she's the most dangerous possibility, we should operate under the assumption it's her," Nash said.

"Agreed." I drummed my fingers on my leg and stared at

the woman for a few more seconds. "If it is Bellarose, she's going to make a move soon, which means we need to go after that book." I turned to Craig. "Anyone suspicious turn up today when you were watching Corville's place?"

"A package was left at the front door. That's it."

"Okay, good." I leaned over Dez's shoulder for a better view of his screen. "Can you walk me through the layout of his house? We need to be ready to hit the place before she beats us to it."

In the end, we decided to give it one more day. Craig assured me that he would make sure Bellarose or anyone else didn't get inside Corville's house before we had a chance to go after the book. According to Kali, the rumor was that Corville's next big party would be tomorrow night. Since I'd be working with him in the morning, I'd try to score an invitation. In an area full of neighborhood watch signs, hitting his place during the day was risky. With a party invite, I could walk out with that spell book without drawing nosy neighbors' attention. Stealing a magical artifact during a house party wasn't ideal, but it might be our best shot. I needed to be prepared if the opportunity presented itself. Worst-case scenario, I could at least locate the book and map the onsite security features and then circle back after the party to take it.

Craig's phone buzzed as we were finishing up, Volkov's name flashing across the screen. "You're on speaker," Craig answered, his phone manners almost as bad as Volkov's.

"I saw a missed call from you," Volkov said. "What is it?"

Craig looked at me as he answered. "Got a call about twenty minutes ago from Martha, the High Priestess of the Kansas City coven, demanding I escort Riley to their headquarters immediately for a mandatory evaluation."

Volkov swore.

"I told her to take it up with you," Craig told him.

This was the first I was hearing about it. "She left a couple voicemails for me today as well," I added. "I ignored them."

"Block her number," Volkov ordered. "I'll deal with it. The witches have no jurisdiction here. You're not in their coven."

"I'll let Helen know Martha's escalating things," I said. Cicadas wouldn't be the only surprises Helen had in store for her.

Before Craig could cut the call, I snagged his phone and took it off speaker, so I could talk to Volkov alone. Although I asked about his mother's visit, he steered the conversation back to me. After rehashing my disaster of a day, I updated him about our plans.

"I'm sorry I'll miss it," he said.

"And here, I didn't think heists were your style," I teased.

"I'm talking about the pool party. Send me a photo, so I don't miss seeing you in a swimsuit."

I laughed. "I'll need to find a swimsuit first."

"Leave that to me," Volkov said. "You wow them on set tomorrow. I'll have something delivered."

The troubles of the day faded, the timbre of his voice stoking something warm and sweet in my chest as we talked late into the night.

CHAPTER 11

"Looks like it's your lucky day, slugger." Monty Corville managed to appear charming despite the salacious wink he shot my way. "I'm a lot sturdier than what's-his-name, so no need to hold back on my account."

Trevor glared at me, as if he just remembered I took out his last stuntman with an elbow strike. Dez's compulsion skills must be improving because Trevor didn't call security.

Corville looked at the stunt coordinator. "I'm surprised he didn't fire you." The interest in his gaze made me wary. If he was a vampire, I couldn't afford for him to see me as a threat and disappear with that artifact.

I bit my lip and scrunched my nose. "He wanted to," I confessed. "I think he felt sorry for me. This is my first big movie." I put as much fresh-off-the-farm wonder into my voice as I could manage. "Any advice for the newbie? I really need this job, or my mom is going to make me move back to Ohio."

Corville rattled off several tips I'd already found online. I hung onto his every word while scanning for any tells that screamed vampire. In person, Corville's brown eyes appeared far lighter than they appeared on the entertainment news clip we'd watched. His body was fit without being bulky, and he had the sun-kissed complexion of a beach lover. Absolutely nothing about him hinted vampire, and yet, I couldn't shake the feeling he was.

After running through the attack scene twice without incident, I decided there was one nearly foolproof way to find out. The next time I got in position for the scene, I used the jagged edge of a metal locker to slice my palm. I pumped my fist a few times to get the blood flowing before I yelped.

"Ouch! Watch out," I warned him, holding my bleeding hand under Corville's nose. "That locker edge is sharp."

His nostrils flared at the scent of blood, but his eyes remained a tranquil brown without a flicker of bloodlust. Unless he was one of the old ones—which the healthy tan belied—no way he could be that close to blood without some kind of reaction.

I guess my vamp radar is as wonky as my magic.

Trevor wrapped my palm with gauze and, despite my objections that it was only a minor cut, insisted I get it checked out on break. Trevor also declared that they had all the footage they needed of the attack scene, which meant two things. One, I'd be back on cheer duty this afternoon. *Yay me.* And two, Monty Corville would go back to his regular gig. My window to snag a party invitation was slamming shut. He might not be a vamp, but that party was my best opportunity to get close to that demon spell book.

"It's been such an honor to work with you," Cradling my hand to my chest, I laid the flattery on thick. "I hope I see you again. I don't know many people in L.A. yet."

He ignored my bloody hand, his gaze dipping to my neck where my pulse raced. Hopefully, he'd chalk it up to nervous attempts at flirting. Corville leaned close enough I could smell his liberal aftershave. "I'm having a pool party tonight. A lot of the cast and crew show up. You should come."

With a big smile, I pulled out my cell phone, quickly swiping past the photo of a vending machine in front of coven headquarters that Helen texted me. "I'd love to. What's your address?" I dutifully typed it in as if my team hadn't spent the past two days casing his place. "Do you mind if I bring a friend?"

Corville flashed me a million-watt smile. "The more pretty girls, the merrier."

Ignoring Trevor's directive to get my already healing palm checked out, I headed for the costume trailer. As I walked, I pulled up Helen's text, captioned "special delivery—Bea's idea" and squinted at the photo. Then I giggled. Instead of candy or pop, the vending machine dispensed an assortment of brightly colored t-shirts with obnoxious sayings on them. The vending machine was strategically placed right next to the coven headquarters' front door. From the looks of the line of people waiting to buy a t-shirt, the vending machine was a hit. The follow-up text Helen sent showed a citation issued to Martha Matthews for a public nuisance violation.

I was busy admiring Bea's handiwork when someone bumped into me from behind, knocking my purse off my shoulder and onto the ground. Turning, I came face-to-face with the blonde who had been slinking around Corville yesterday. She was wearing the same red scarf and oversized sunglasses. I checked to find the quartz bracelet on her wrist.

"I'm so sorry!" She bent down to help me pick up the scattered contents of my purse. Her blonde hair was a shade too light, and her lilting voice sounded nothing like Bellarose.

A hookup then. I took the granola bar she handed me with a grateful smile. The tension bled from my muscles, and my step was lighter as I made my way to Kali.

I filled Kali in on my morning, including ruling out Zara Bellarose lurking on set. Without Bellarose chasing our prize, it took some of the pressure off. Instead of a rush job, we could use tonight's party to set up the heist. Then the team could draw Corville out the following night, while I circled back to snatch the artifact without the complications of a house full of party guests.

For once, a job was shaping up to be easier than anticipated. We'd probably even have time for sightseeing.

The fact that Monty Corville was human simplified things as well. I told Kali as much. "Based on Corville's lack of reaction to my blood, it's safe to say, he's not a vamp."

"I'm not so sure about that," Kali argued. "Wait here." She hustled to the other side of the room to get something. When she returned, she handed me a box of contacts.

I looked at her blankly.

"Those are brown contacts. No prescription, purely cosmetic." She tapped the box. "Monty Corville has Stella special order them for him."

"Okay." I handed the box back to her. "Why is that relevant? A lot of people wear contacts to change their eye color." My stomach clenched thinking about how my own mother had been one of them.

"Exactly," Kali said. "But here's the weird thing. Monty Corville's natural eye color is—wait for it—brown."

I whistled. "Vampire."

She nodded. "With those contacts in, his eyes could be ruby red with bloodlust, and you'd never know it."

Suddenly, his fixation on my pulse earlier made sense. There went my easy job stealing from a human. "At least we know what we're dealing with," I said.

Because Corville was a vampire, he'd know what that spell book was capable of. Plus, I'd have to coordinate with Craig who was charged with taking Corville out. As a supernatural, Corville would no doubt have the book warded. Fortunately, those null powers of mine would prove useful.

I grabbed a tropical bikini off a rack and tossed it to Kali. "You're going to need this because tonight, we're invited to Corville's latest pool bash. We'll have a drink, hit a beach ball around, and figure out how to steal that book out from under his undead nose. But first, I need to survive this afternoon."

Kali frowned and put the bikini back on the rack. "What's this afternoon?"

"Cheerleading."

Turns out, online videos don't make the best cheer coaches. Half a dozen botched stunts later, I was huddled in an alcove speed dialing Dez. I had to call twice before he picked up. "How many times can you compel someone to give me my job back before you risk permanent brain damage?" I asked.

"No clue." He didn't sound overly concerned.

Surely, it was more than two. It'd probably be fine. Besides, unless tonight was a total bust, we'd likely only have a couple more days on set. At least tomorrow we were filming a stabbing scene. I was confident I'd be better at that.

Dez's compulsion skills were definitely improving. With little effort, he convinced Trevor that he hadn't, in fact, fired me. I filled everyone in as Dez drove us back to the rental house.

When we got there, a nondescript brown package sat on the porch. Kali picked up and examined it. "Special delivery." She tossed it to me. "Why is Volkov sending you mail?"

"I mentioned I didn't have a swimsuit for the pool party." I fought the smile at the outrageous amount he must have paid to have this shipped overnight to me.

Nash went inside, not at all interested in the big reveal. Kali and Dez, however, angled for a better look.

Dez eyed the package and whistled. "Oh, this should be good. I'm guessing a gold string bikini." He wiggled his eyebrows. "Princess Leia and Jabba the Hutt style."

Kali laughed. "You're such a nerd."

Dez made a face. "You say that as if it's a bad thing."

Kali studied the package I held. "You're also wrong about the bikini. That man is so buttoned-up, I'll bet he sent a full-coverage one piece in a tasteful navy."

I shook my head at their commentary and ripped the package open, anticipation rising. The suit inside was neither a gold bikini nor a conservative one piece. It was a black two-piece you could dive into a pool wearing without fearing you'd lose the bottoms. But it was the top that made me grin like a fool. The cropped tank had a single chunky shoulder strap and a neon pink anarchy symbol stamped across the front. "It's perfect."

"Huh." Kali leaned closer, looking impressed. "It really is."

We had enough time to order pizza and finalize our plan before we needed to change into swimwear. After coordinating pizza topping requests with everyone, I found a local place that delivered and typed in the online order. Until I started working for the Enclave, I'd operated on a cash-only basis. Carrying a bank card and an unwieldy purse along with it took some getting used to. I rifled through the contents of my purse but came up empty-handed.

"Anyone see my bank card?" I hoped I hadn't left it lying on the ground where I'd spilled my purse on set.

After a lot of digging, I finally found the card in a side pocket. My relief, however, was short-lived when I pulled out the object next to it. I might not be a model witch, but even I knew a hex charm when I saw it.

CHAPTER 12

If the magical symbol carved into the stone hadn't clued me in, the malevolent glow certainly would have. I examined the hex charm. While I could see the magic pulsing around it, I didn't have a clue what it did. Because I wasn't willing to risk the hex affecting the others, I isolated myself in the bedroom and called Helen.

"I need your expertise," I said.

"Sure, hon. What do you need to know?" Helen propped the phone up, giving me a view of both her and Bea.

"You want to know how to reel in those California boys, right?" Bea made a motion like she was reeling in a fishing line before winking at me. "Don't you worry. I've got you, doll."

Before she could launch into seduction tips, I held up the charm. "Not that kind of expertise, Bea. I need to know what this hex does."

Both women stilled.

"Where did you get that?" Helen asked.

"A witch slipped it in my purse without me noticing." I

cringed. "I should've been paying more attention." Apparently, I was better at pickpocketing than safeguarding a purse.

Helen picked up Garth and settled him on her lap like he was a cat. "Let's see it then."

I held the charm closer to the camera. "Do you recognize this?" The symbol etched into the slate gray stone had eight arrows radiating from a central point.

Because she steadfastly refused to wear reading glasses, Bea squinted to see it. "Chaos star."

Helen nodded.

I frowned. Chaos could mean a lot of things. "What does it do?"

"With a hex charm, the symbol is only one part of the magic," Helen explained. "Hexes, like most spells, are driven by intention. Without knowing the witch's intention or at least the ritual used to create the charm, all I can do is guess based on the materials she constructed it with. Can you flip it over and show me the back?"

I did as she asked.

"From the looks of it, the bezel cup is made of iron. That's fairly common for hex charms." Helen gestured for me to turn it over again. "The stone cabochon is hematite. It's typically used to protect personal spaces like your home or car. Paired with the chaos symbol, my best guess is that it's some kind of confounding hex, probably meant to prevent you from entering a space. Most people carrying an object with a confounding hex will be confused, lost even, if they approach wherever it's anchored to."

I stared at the charm. "A space like Monty Corville's house."

"Makes sense," Bea agreed.

"Is there a way to neutralize this thing?" I ran my finger

over the smooth surface of the stone, feeling the magical charge brushing against my skin. "It won't work on me, but I won't be the only one going to Corville's house to get the demon spell book. I'd rather not risk leaving it lying around."

Garth stopped fussing with his feathers long enough to crow, his beady red eyes staring intently into the camera. I might not speak chicken, but I could empathize with the urge to scream. "You're telling me, buddy."

When he continued crowing, Helen set him on the floor with a chicken toy filled with treats. "Most witches could do a counter spell," she said.

"But I'm not most witches," I finished. "What should I do?"

"You got a hammer?" Helen asked. "Smashing it to bits should do the trick. Normally, I wouldn't advise it since the magical kickback can be dangerous, but for you, it'll be harmless."

At least my null ability would be useful. "Works for me." I should see the magic dissipate, so I'd be able to make sure it was no longer a danger to the others.

Helen's eyes narrowed. "Now tell me about this witch who hexed you."

"There's not a lot to tell. She was blonde, a little taller than me, but she was wearing a scarf and big sunglasses so I couldn't make out her features. I'm just glad she wasn't Bellarose like I initially suspected."

Bea tilted her head. "Are you sure? Don't be so quick to dismiss her. Zara Bellarose is a master illusionist, after all."

She had a point, but my gut said it wasn't Bellarose. "Do illusion spells normally alter someone's voice?"

"None that I know of," Helen said.

"Then yes, I'm sure."

After ending the call, I went in search of a hammer. I had

to settle for a meat tenderizer I found in a kitchen drawer. Ten minutes later, the rest of my team was crowded around the shattered hex charm.

Nash stared down at the busted stone while running his fingers over the charm he wore around his own neck. Helen and the girls made it for him and spelled it to look like a tacky shark-tooth necklace. In reality, it disguised a chip of the Alatyr stone that made Nash virtually indestructible. When he caught me watching, he dropped the necklace and cleared his throat. "The question is, who is the witch working with—Corville or someone else gunning for that book?"

"I guess we'll find out tonight when we see how surprised he is when I show up for his party. If the witch is working with Corville, he already knows what I'm after. And if she's working with another interested party, they'll think their hex took me out of commission. Hopefully, they won't be in a hurry to nab the book. Either way, we need to go after it tonight." I looked at Craig. "Anyone suspicious coming or going from Corville's place today?"

"I set up discreet cameras yesterday, so Dez and I could monitor the house around the clock. I didn't see anyone this morning." Craig turned to Dez. "What about you?"

"No one suspicious," Dez said. "The only person I saw was a pool maintenance guy who fished out some debris and topped up the pool chemicals."

My shoulders relaxed a fraction. "Good. Can you show me the media clip of Corville's party?" I asked Dez. "I need to see that display case he's keeping the spell book in."

Dez pulled up the footage and paused it.

I studied the setup. "Most people would lock something this valuable in a safe. But Monty Corville loves to show off, and that's going to work in our favor." I pointed to the glass protecting the artifact. "This is museum-quality glass, which means reinforced and shatterproof. Not impossible to break but difficult enough to be a deterrent. However, the display case is mounted on the antique library table. See the steel housing at the base of the glass where it's attached to the table? There's a locking mechanism there. I'd also bet it has motion sensors on the tabletop around the exterior, so if someone attempts to pry the glass off, it'll set off an alarm."

Everyone was frowning at me.

Dez rubbed his cheek. "How does that work in our favor? If you break the glass, won't those tabletop sensors go off?"

"Yup." I grinned. "But I won't be breaking glass." I tapped the library table on screen. "I'll go through the underside of the table. All I need is a compact battery-operated circular saw with a fine-toothed blade. I'll cut through the table, grab the book through the opening, and waltz out with my prize." As a bonus, I could use the saw for headquarters' improvement projects when we got back to Kansas City.

"Won't people hear the saw?" Kali asked.

"Hopefully not with the party going full swing. Dez, do you have any of that potion left you used on the drone?"

He frowned. "Yeah, but won't you duddify it?"

"Duddify?" Nash sneered. "That's not even a word."

I tugged Dez around to face me before he argued with Nash. "As long as I wear gloves, it should work."

"Should being the operative word there," Nash pointed out.

"No risk, no reward," I countered. "I'm also going to need to keep Corville out of the house. Kali, that's where you come in. I need a distraction."

She perked up. "Beer Pong?"

"It pains me to say it, but no beer pong." I hit play on the video, and we watched Corville pander to the crowd. "You said Stella told you that Corville's schtick is diving off the balcony to kick off his parties, right?"

Kali nodded. "He's a real drama llama."

He definitely was. "The spell book is located on the second-floor landing, next to the bedroom with the balcony overlooking the pool. First, I need you to distract Corville long enough I can slip upstairs and hide in the bedroom closet."

"Distract how?" Craig grumbled.

Kali patted Craig's arm. "With an ego like his, I'll get him talking about himself."

Mollified, Craig motioned for me to continue.

"When Corville comes up for his nightly showboating, Kali, you can lead the jump chant from poolside. As soon as he dives, you'll give me the green light, and I'll make my move. While everyone parties with Corville in the backyard, I'll have plenty of time to steal that book."

"How are you going to get it out of the house?" Dez asked.

I patted my swim bag. "The same way I'll be getting the saw in. Wrapped in a big ol' beach towel. As long as the witch isn't working with Corville, this should be an easy in-and-out job."

Nash crossed his arms over his chest. "And if he is working with her? Then what?"

"In that case, I'm going to need a bigger distraction to get inside. Got any ideas?"

Nash's eyes lit up. "One. But I'll need to commandeer Dez's invisible drone."

CHAPTER 13

The party was in full swing when Kali and I arrived right before dusk. Nash was giving us a ten-minute head start before sweet talking his way in, so we wouldn't be seen together. Because he worked on set as security, we assumed he'd blend in with the cast and crew. Of course, that was before seeing the ratio of bikini-clad women to men.

Most of the yard was dedicated to the gorgeous zero-edge pool that nearly spanned the width of the house. The swimming pool had all the bells and whistles, from colored LED lights and a smoky blue mood fog to a full sound system playing beach tunes. A narrow concrete walkway bordered by a tall green privacy hedge was on one side of the pool. On the other, large concrete pavers with deep green moss growing in the gaps provided space for the open bar and limited seating.

No one seemed to mind standing as they clustered in small groups, wine glasses and bottles of craft beer in hand. Large sliding glass doors opened onto the patio, with finger foods artfully arranged on the dining room table inside. Few people were eating though, which told me that this definitely was not my kind of crowd.

No one was in the pool yet, presumably waiting for Monty Corville's big entrance. He was nowhere in sight. Although there were plenty of blondes mingling, none of them wore scarves, and no one looked surprised to see me. Either the witch who hexed me had a world-class poker face, or she wasn't here. *Fingers crossed for the latter.* Barring talking to every blonde until I recognized her voice, I'd have to take my chances.

As we wove our way through the crowded backyard, I recognized a few familiar faces, including Kelsey from the stunt team. When she spotted me, she scowled. I gave her a jaunty little finger wave until Kali elbowed me in the gut. "Oof. What did you do that for?"

Kali held her finger up. "Stop antagonizing the cheerleader."

"She's not a real cheerleader, but fine." I nudged her as I scanned the people around us. "Why is everyone wearing makeup to a pool party?"

"Maybe they're not planning on swimming."

"Then why come?" I asked.

She slid her sunglasses down her nose, so I could see her eye shadow. It was tastefully applied, but a total waste of time. "To be seen, obviously," she said.

I pointed at her eyelids. "That's going to wash off in the pool," I warned her. "Plus, you're wearing sunglasses. No one can even see it."

Kali sighed and slid the glasses on top of her head. "I'll keep my head above water, but this suit—" She swept a hand down her body, "deserves the full makeup treatment."

We probably made an odd duo—me in my punk rock

anarchy suit and bright pink hair and Kali in her cute retro bikini. She wore black and white polka dot bottoms and a cherry red halter top that looked amazing next to that mass of curly, dark hair.

"Plus, Raum wants to come out to play," she admitted. For a second, her brown eyes turned demon black before she slid the sunglasses back into place. Despite Kali's impressive control over the demon tethered to her soul, Raum occasionally pushed his way to the surface. "I think it's the book," she whispered. "It's like his version of catnip."

Monty Corville's booming voice cut off my reply. "Rachel, glad you could make it." Corville intercepted us, never taking his eyes off Kali. "Introduce me to your friend."

I pointed to myself. "It's Riley." I don't know why I bothered. Corville paid no attention to me. "And this is my friend Kali, who works on the costume team at the studio."

Corville's gaze swept down her body, lingering on the halter top, his smile hungry. "I'm not surprised. I can see you have excellent fashion sense, Kali."

I pressed my lips together to stop the snarky retort. From his blatant disinterest in me, I was guessing the witch wasn't working for him. I scanned the area again for the blonde witch but didn't see anyone who stood out. "Kali, I'm going to get us some drinks. You good here?"

Now that Corville was eyeing Kali like a snack, I regretted my decision to leave my dagger at the rental. Sadly, swimwear didn't have many options for hiding a demon blade capable of killing vampires. Maybe I should have smuggled it in my swim bag. I narrowed my eyes at Corville. In a pinch, the portable saw would probably work to take his head off, but it'd be messy.

Kali pokedT me in the side and flicked her gaze to the

house. "Peachy. I'll catch up with you in a bit." She smiled up at Corville. "And you are?" she asked, the hint of Raum in her husky voice reminding me she could handle herself.

Corville launched into a well-rehearsed pickup spiel as I headed toward the house, my oversized pool bag heavy on my shoulder. After snagging a few appetizers, I asked a trio of women to point me to the bathroom, even though I knew exactly where it was thanks to Dez's recon. I smiled and thanked them before making my way upstairs, pausing on the large landing to admire the demon spell book that brought me here.

Because of the way the stairs were positioned off to one side of the landing, the antique table that held the main attraction wasn't visible from the first floor, giving me the privacy I'd need to steal it. Behind the table, a large window framed the book and the view of the city beyond it. Track lighting illuminated the display case and, beneath it, a book so dangerous it warranted a kill order for flaunting it.

The spell book appeared ancient, its text unlike any I'd seen. As a thief for Carl, I'd come across my share of dead languages, but demon wasn't among them. The script was more elegant than I'd expected demon writing to be. Then again, evil often masqueraded in pretty packaging.

Not willing to risk setting off a motion alarm, I kept my distance as I surveyed the area. As I suspected, there were ample wards surrounding the book. I might not be able to cast a spell, but I was about to put that null ability to good use. Long before I had a name for what I was, my ability to circumvent magic granted me an edge as a thief. Supernaturals often skimped on human security features, trusting their magic to safeguard their treasures. From the looks of this setup, Monty Corville was no different.

Based on the slight wear on the floorboard in front of the display, people frequently stopped to admire the book. That meant no motion sensors, with the exception of possible tabletop sensors around the glass display case. Because the table was backed by windows, there was no place to attach a sensor that would trigger an alarm if the book was moved. Thanks to Corville's subpar security features, the whole job should take ten minutes, tops.

When I heard voices on the stairs, I made a break for the master bedroom, tucking myself into the closet. For the next ten minutes, I practiced slowing my breathing and calming my heart rate, like Carl drilled into me years ago. Ninety percent of success as a thief relied on a clear head and steady nerves. Although I hated waiting, I'd learned how to manage it. Box breathing helped. Breathe in, count to four. Hold for four. Exhale for four. Hold for four. Repeat.

Kali's voice broke my concentration. "He's on his way." The comms we all wore tonight were as small as earbuds, but because they used technology that captured speech from inside the ear canal, they eliminated the need for mics. Dez scored us the coolest toys.

"I'm in position. Nash?"

"Yeah. I've got you covered if you need a distraction to get out." Nash sounded hopeful that he'd get to buzz the crowd with his invisible drone.

I smiled and then settled in for the wait. It wasn't long before I heard Corville enter the bedroom, followed by the slide of the balcony door. With that door open, I heard the chants of the crowd urging Corville to jump. I rolled my shoulders. *Go time.*

"Now!" Kali said as the cheers died down.

I opened the closet door to a momentary lull. Before I

could cross the room, a woman screamed. The sound of a panicking crowd drew me to the balcony. I stopped abruptly when I saw why they were screaming. Monty Corville floated face-down in the pool. That wasn't the worst of it. His body disintegrated before my eyes. People scrambled away, bumping into each other and knocking over patio chairs in their haste to put distance between them and whatever was in that water.

"What the hell just happened?" I stepped onto the balcony for a better look. Dropping my swim bag on a nearby chair, I leaned over the railing and stared at the smoky blue haze rising from the water like fog, no sign of Corville beneath it.

"Someone called 911," Nash warned. "Get a move on it, Cruz. You've got minutes before cops swarm this place."

"You and Kali, get out," I said. "I'll meet you back at the rental. Craig, you there big guy?"

"I'm here," he said. "Open the side window when you've got the book. I'm on the roof."

I thanked the universe for the modern lines and flat roof of Corville's house that was capable of hiding a man who could fly us out of here if need be. It was almost fully dark now. Hopefully, that would give us enough cover that no one would see him leaping into the sky.

"Will do." One last look at the pool, and my stomach pitched. It hit me why no one else was staring at the blue haze. I was the only one who could see it. *Magic.*

That meant the witch was not only here, she was also one step ahead of me. The only reason to kill Corville with a backyard full of witnesses was to create a distraction big enough to steal that artifact. *Shit.* I shouldn't have allowed myself to get distracted.

Before I could turn around to go after the spell book,

strong arms banded around my legs and lifted me, tossing me over the balcony railing toward the death magic still swirling in the pool below. Plunging into a swimming pool that disintegrated a human body might be a foolproof way to test my null abilities, but it was also guaranteed to warrant police questioning.

If I survived.

CHAPTER 14

My body slammed into the concrete balcony as I clung to the railing. The pain made my breath catch and my palm slip, the bottom rail all that prevented me from plummeting to the death pool below. *Was this my penance for busting that stunt guy's rib?* I dangled precariously, which inspired a fresh bout of screaming from the people fleeing the scene.

I tuned them out to concentrate on getting a firmer hold before reaching for the top railing. It was too far for me to grab. After years of bartending and karaoke, I was going soft. Back in the day, I conditioned like my life depended on it because it had. At the moment, the muscles in my upper body burned as I attempted to pull myself up and swing my leg onto the ledge. My body trembled with the effort, but my grip was too precarious to maintain the position long enough to gain a foothold. Looked like my fancy new bar would have to wait since workout equipment just skyrocketed to the top of my headquarters' renovation wish list.

Since I couldn't power myself up, I tried another tactic.

One hand at a time, I reached through the metal spindles to the elbow, gripping the farthest one I could. Once I managed a firm hold and a clear view of the second floor beyond the balcony, I scanned for my attacker. A figure in head-to-toe black combat clothes rushed to the stairs. From the build, the attacker was male. There was no way I'd reach him in time to stop him, but at least he hadn't stuck around to stomp on my fingers.

Unfortunately, he wasn't working alone. While I clung to the railing, his accomplice prepared to finish what he started. Unlike her partner, the woman didn't bother hiding her face, which made her easily recognizable as the witch who hexed me. From the way she drew the air around her to form a miniature tornado on her left palm, hexing wasn't her only skill.

"You shouldn't be here." She tilted her head to study me. "What are you?"

I inched my way up the railing. "Tougher than I look."

"The hex—," she said.

"Beginner?" I ventured. "I'm sure you'll get better at it with practice." *Unless I catch you before you escape,* I thought.

She narrowed her eyes at the insult. With her free hand, the witch tossed blue powder into the vortex and mumbled a quick incantation too low for me to make out the words. She hurled the magic at me with a flick of her wrist.

I braced for impact. Even if Helen's null theory proved correct, I'd only be immune to whatever nasty magic she'd activated with that powder. Air was air though. It hit me with enough force to blow my hair back and make my eyes water. The magic skated across my skin and left a bitter taste on my tongue when I breathed it in. I sure hoped those null abilities extended to vital organs—like lungs. The witch's eyes widened, a spark of interest in her gaze. When frightened voices drifted up to us. she shot me one last look before abandoning me to follow her partner.

When the air dissipated, I threw a leg onto the railing and hoisted myself up and then over it. I landed on my feet, but by the witch was gone, a haze of blue smoke where she stood.

Because she'd been both empty-handed and identifiable, I focused on her partner, crossing my fingers that I'd interrupted him before he had time to steal that artifact. "Craig, I need you to stop the guy in black running from the house."

"Dozens of people are running from that house screaming right now," he pointed out. "You're going to have to be more specific."

I gritted my teeth. "He'll be the one not in a swimsuit. He's wearing full coverage black clothing. Should be easy to spot in this crowd." I hurried toward the demon spell book with a thudding heart and dread pooling in my gut. Gone. They hadn't bothered with finesse. I kicked what was left of the display case. "And he'll be carrying my book."

Craig swore. "I don't see anyone matching that description."

The man must have slipped past Craig while the witch stuck around to finish me off. "He's working with the woman who hexed me," I added. Since I'd already described her to the team, Craig would know who he was looking for. If he caught her, she could lead us straight to her partner and—more importantly—the artifact.

"On it," he said. "Now get out of there. I see squad cars closing in. Go out the front door, turn left, and stop behind the green SUV parked down the street. I'll circle back for you after I sweep the area."

I grabbed my swim bag and joined the swarm of party

guests racing from Corville's place. Although I watched the skies, expecting Craig to drop from above, he was on foot when he arrived at our meetup spot. He was also alone. By the time we made it back to the rental, the adrenaline had worn off, and my whole body hurt.

Kali met us at the door. "Are you okay?" she asked me, staring at the mottled bruise on my side that a two-piece swimsuit did nothing to hide. Kali waited for my nod before moving on to Craig. She didn't ask him if he was okay, but she ran her hands over his torso to check for injuries. The man was as sturdy as a stone wall, but that didn't stop her from worrying.

Satisfied that we were both unharmed, she retreated to the living room where Dez and Nash both waited. Nash's rigid posture relaxed when he caught sight of me. As usual, Dez's laptop was open, and once he assured himself that I was okay, his attention returned to his screen.

"I'm pulling up the camera footage to search for our guy now," he said.

Thanks to our comms, Dez heard the description I gave Craig. Unless my attacker ditched his black attire before leaving the house, Dez would have no trouble identifying him.

I rotated my shoulder, wincing at the ache. "Good. See if you can get a still of the witch I described. She'll be close on his heels."

Dez nodded and got back to work.

Before Nash could play twenty questions, I held up a hand. "Shower first, then we'll regroup."

No one argued.

In the bathroom, I stripped off my swimsuit and turned the shower on full blast, making it as hot as I could tolerate. Ten minutes under scalding water eased my knotted muscles and cleared my head. I made a pit stop in my bedroom long enough to put on loose sweats.

Everyone was in the kitchen when I returned, Dez's laptop and the dossier on the movie crew spread across the table. I dropped into an empty chair and told them about the attack before turning to Dez.

"It's a start. You saw what happened to Corville?" I asked.

"I did," Dez said. "As far as distractions go, it was efficient."

"Saves me from taking him out," Craig added.

"Did you spot the attacker?"

"I did." Dez flipped the laptop around and pointed to a blurry image of the guy. With a black ski mask obscuring the man's features, the picture did us little good.

"And the witch?" I asked.

Dez opened another image, this one clearer. Unfortunately, she'd kept her head down and snug against her shoulder. Dez frowned. "I'm running her through facial recognition software now, but with a partial face, we're likely to get a lot of hits."

My stomach rumbled. I grabbed a banana from the counter and peeled it while I tried to recall something about the attacker that could help identify him. The man was average in height and build. His clothes were all nondescript black. Because I'd only glimpsed his retreating back, I couldn't even pin down an eye color. I took an aggressive bite of banana. There had to be something. "The pool."

"What about it?" Dez asked.

I tossed my empty peel in the trash and pointed to Dez's laptop. "Can you pull up the footage of the witch when she was by the pool?"

Dez frowned. "She wasn't anywhere near the pool." He zoomed in to the still he'd taken of her to show the background. "She came in through the front door, and she didn't show up on any of the backyard drone footage Nash took."

The blue fog. I snapped my fingers and grinned.

"Why are you smiling?" Dez asked.

Nash answered, picking up on the same thing I had. "If the witch didn't slip the magic in the pool during the party, it was already there."

Craig tensed. "The pool maintenance guy."

I nodded. "Exactly." Dez, can you pull up the video that shows the pool guy topping up the chorine?"

"Sure thing."

A few minutes later, Dez stopped the video on a man of average height and build emptying a small container directly into the pool. On camera, I couldn't see the magic, but I had no doubt that's what it was. Apparently, my ability to see magic didn't extend to video.

Everyone leaned in for a closer look at our guy. He wore a baseball cap, but a good portion of his lower face was visible. The man was clean-shaven with a soft jaw and unremarkable nose. He looked like a dozen men I'd passed on the street just this week.

"There," Nash pointed at the man's bicep where his short-sleeved shirt rode up. Black ink peeked out.

Dez zoomed in for a better look at the tattoo.

I squinted. Only half of it was visible, and the tattoo seemed to be random shapes. One side was a straight line with three rectangular legs on the bottom, each of which was split with a line and circle on top. The other side looked like a toddler's scribbling. "What do you think that is?"

Everyone shrugged.

"A bad drawing of an elephant," Kali guessed.

"Whatever it is," Dez said. "It's unique enough to be identifiable." He saved the image. "I'll run him through facial recognition as well and see what comes up."

An hour later, we had over a hundred matches for our witch and seventy-six for my attacker. With that many suspects to wade through, we wouldn't be tracking down either of them tonight.

Dez confirmed it. "I'll dig up photos and addresses for everyone I can, but with this many, it's going to take a while."

"How long is a while?" Nash asked.

Dez raked a hand through his hair. "A few days, most likely."

Nash sighed. "He could be anywhere by then."

Dez stiffened. "You got a better idea?"

"No," Nash admitted.

"All right, then. Let's pack up tonight," I said. "We can hunt for a needle in a haystack from home tomorrow as easily as we could from here."

CHAPTER 15

After a botched burglary and a flight, all I wanted was a salty snack and an early afternoon nap, in that order. Whoever was incessantly ringing my doorbell had other ideas.

"Coming!" I yelled, forcing myself out of the bed I'd just settled into with my bag of pretzels. I looked out the peephole and groaned. Maybe if I ignored her, she'd go away.

When she abandoned the doorbell to pound on the door, I figured I might as well get this over with. I unlatched the dead bolt and opened the door enough for a conversation but not wide enough to be mistaken for an invitation.

"Martha." I greeted the middle-aged woman poised with her fist in the air.

She dropped her hand to her side and forced a smile that looked as fake as that knock-off purse on her shoulder. It dimmed when she caught sight of my ratty Nirvana shirt, comfy sleep shorts, and messy pink hair. Unlike me, Martha wore a power suit and sensible heels, her ash brown hair in a perfect bob. She looks like a realtor. The only things remotely witchy about her were the amulet around her neck and the heavy scent of lavender that clung to her skin.

"Riley Cruz?" she asked, as if we hadn't met a dozen times over the years.

We may not run in the same circles, but the Kansas City supernatural community was small enough that it was impossible to avoid coven leadership entirely. Plus, this woman popped into the Stitch Witch at least once a year to try to coerce Helen and the girls back into the fold. Not that she ever made any headway.

"That's me." I glanced at the two yes-ma'am witches who flanked her. I didn't know either by name, but I'd seen them around—usually lockstep with Martha. Both wore flowing dresses and enough crystals to stock a small store. Neither of them smiled. "What can I do for you, Martha?"

She pursed her lips. "I presume you got my voicemails?"

"Sorry. I've been on a job," I said diplomatically, not mentioning that I deleted all but the first one without listening to them.

"Well," she huffed. "Since you haven't had good role models, you may not be aware of the expectations."

I raised a brow. "Expectations?"

"Yes. Expectations." She said the word slowly like she suspected I was unfamiliar with it. "As the head of the coven, you answer to me."

I snorted. "I don't think so."

The two women with Martha stiffened. Martha, however, smiled. "Oh, you do, child. The second you displayed even a flicker of magic, you became my problem. That means, you return my calls promptly and come when I request your presence. Since you've avoided my calls, I was forced to come to you. Do you understand how many responsibilities I juggle? I do not have time for these games." She snapped her fingers in front of my face and pointed to my apartment. "Now go get dressed in something appropriate, so we can begin the evaluation."

I laughed. "Thanks, but I'm gonna pass. I'm a shifter, which means I don't answer to you." I didn't answer to Volkov either, but I left that part unsaid.

"A shifter with magic," she countered. "An untrained witch is a dangerous witch."

The two women nodded.

"Listen, if you don't like it, take it up with the Tribunal. I hear they handle these types of disputes," I suggested.

"Max Volkov is stonewalling me," she snapped. "He's suddenly requiring a formal request for an audience like he's a king." Her eyes flashed with outrage. "From what I hear, his refusal to stand down is due to a conflict of interest since you are seeing the alpha." She gave me another once over, her brows pinched as if trying to figure out how that happened.

Volkov's inability to back down went far beyond me, but in this case, I appreciated that stubbornness more than usual. I smiled sweetly at the women. "Red tape is a real bitch, isn't it?"

I tried to close the door, but Martha wedged her foot in to hold it open, the scent of lavender so strong it made my eyes water. From the frown lines etched into her forehead, it'd take more than bathing in an herb to calm her down when dealing with me. I stared at her shoe. "Really?" Short of slamming the door on her foot, we were at a standstill. I opened the door wider and waited for her to give up and go home. "I'm not going to change my mind."

Martha squared her shoulders. "You've forced my hand." She rooted around in her purse, pulling out a small pamphlet marked with colorful tabs. She opened it on the green tab and cleared her throat. "Article III, Section IV." Martha looked up to make sure she had my full attention, then nodded to the brunette on her right before continuing. "Any unaffiliated witch living in the greater Kansas City area shall be subject to the jurisdiction of the Kansas City Coven of the Divine Sisterhood of Sacred Truth until such time that the witch is deemed sufficiently trained and non-dangerous to the public."

I couldn't help but snicker. "That's a real mouthful." No wonder Helen and the girls steered clear. If the coven's full name was that pompous, I bet they were sticklers for parliamentary procedure at all those monthly meetings.

Martha snapped the pamphlet shut and pointed at me. "You are an unaffiliated witch."

"Alleged," I corrected, kicking her foot out of the doorway.

Before I could slam the door in their faces, the brunette grabbed my left wrist and slapped a cuff on it before reaching for my right hand. I held my arm above my head and out of her reach. "What are you doing?"

"Since you won't come willingly, then I have no choice but to force your compliance," Martha said, a grim smile on her lips. "You can make this easy on yourself and allow Alona to put the magic-canceling handcuffs on you, or I can force that as well."

There might be three of them, but I'd lay money on none of them having fight skills. But Martha wasn't talking about physical force. She hit me with an incapacitation spell that did jack diddly. Neither the cuffs nor her little incantation could hold me, but Helen's warning rang in my ears.

If Martha learned I was a null, it'd be far worse than going along with her little dog and pony show. So, I forced myself to still, and allowed Alona to yank my arm down and secure the remaining cuff. Better to go along with this and suffer an hour of magical testing than give the coven a reason to declare me a threat and lock me down for good.

"Now then," Martha said after releasing the incapacitation spell. "Let's get you back to coven headquarters, so I can begin the formal evaluation process."

I groaned. Process sounded far longer than an hour. "Will there be snacks?" I asked, thinking about Janis' sugar cookies after the last round of magical testing I suffered through.

"What?" Martha grimaced.

"At the evaluation. Tell me you have decent snacks, at least."

Alona cracked a smile but hid it before Martha noticed.

"We have a juice bar," Martha said grudgingly.

Juice did not qualify as a snack. I dug a stick of cinnamon gum out of my jean's pocket and put it in my mouth. "Hmm. I heard that juice bar got shut down for health violations."

Martha shot me a dirty look before turning her back on me and marching outside, relying on her minions to ensure I trailed after her like a well-trained puppy. I leaned closer to Alona, "You think you can score me something that requires chewing?"

This time, she kept a straight face. "Salty or sweet?"

I stared at Martha's retreating back. "Definitely salty."

Although I'd pegged Martha for a minivan driver, she unlocked a late model Land Rover and opened the back door, waiting until Alona and I were seated to close the door and climb in the passenger seat. The remaining witch took the driver's seat.

"Nice wheels." I eyed the thick windows and whistled. "Is that bullet-proof glass?"

"Of course, it is," Martha snapped.

No one talked for the remainder of the ride to coven headquarters. I used the quiet time to strategize how best to avoid outing myself as a null. If Martha declared me a magical dud, I could get back to my life and to hunting artifacts. All I needed to do was keep my head down and my temper in check. Easy.

After a guided tour of coven headquarters and two hours of paperwork and a general health physical, I wasn't so sure. At the moment, I sat on a cot in a small room that reminded me of my elementary school nurse's office—dimly lit, sterile, and uninviting. Without a word to me, the nurse conducting my physical finished her notes and handed them to Martha, who had been supervising the poking and prodding, before leaving us alone.

I held a cotton ball to the spot where the nurse had drawn blood and hoped that null abilities didn't show up on a standard blood test. "Can we get to the magical testing part, so I can go home?"

Martha finished scanning my medical notes before answering. "Formal evaluation is a comprehensive process, Riley."

Unease churned in my gut. "How comprehensive?"

Martha finally looked me in the eye. "We'll begin with a basic magical aptitude test this afternoon. Once I have a baseline for you, we'll move on to skill acquisition and evaluation."

I frowned. "How long will that take?"

"It's hard to say. A few days or a week for the initial testing."

"Initial?" I stood, the magic canceling handcuffs still on my wrists. "I have a job, Martha. You can't keep me here indefinitely."

"Actually, I can." She pivoted on her heel before I could argue and left the room, locking the door behind her.

CHAPTER 16

Some of my greatest assets were thick wrists and small hands. Over the years, they'd gotten me out of my share of handcuffs. Unfortunately, the magic-canceling properties of these cuffs relied on skin contact, which meant Alona had tightened them snugly against my wrists to prevent me from using my so-called magical powers to get out of them. Magic wasn't the only way to ditch handcuffs though. I kicked off the shoes Martha generously let me put on before dragging me down here, slid the shorts down my legs, and shifted into my goat.

I left the still-locked cuffs on the cot, along with a note to Martha with two words—Can you? I added a smiley face, which I was certain she'd read as the middle finger I intended it to be. Then I scrambled through the window I'd opened a few minutes ago, carrying my clothes between my teeth, along with the twenty-dollar bill I'd lifted off the nurse when she took my blood pressure.

I ducked behind a dumpster a block away to shift back and get dressed. Since Martha hadn't let me bring my phone, I couldn't call for a ride, but twenty bucks was more than enough for bus fare. My apartment was the first place Martha would look once she discovered me gone, and the Stitch Witch was the second. Even though it took three buses, a half-a-mile hike from the last bus stop, and almost two hours, I went straight to Volkov's house instead.

After ringing his doorbell, I ran my fingers through my hair and straightened my ratty t-shirt. Not really the homecoming I'd hoped for. It wasn't until the door swung open that I remembered Max might not be home alone.

If it weren't for those stark blue eyes, I wouldn't have recognized the stunning woman who opened the door as Max's mother. Irina Volkov was a couple inches taller than I was, blonde, and elegant in that way of old money. I bit back my groan and forced a polite smile, trying not to cringe at the horrible first impression I was making.

"Hi," I said too cheerfully. "Is Max here?"

Irina gave me a not-so-subtle once over, pausing on the jewel flower tattoo snaking down my leg before meeting my eyes. Her tailored clothes and the classical music drifting through the open door compounded my discomfort. Never had I felt more out of my depth than standing here in front of Max Volkov's mother, waiting to see if she'd let me in.

"This is not a good time for the alpha." She managed to inject a note of censure in the way she said alpha while still sounding polite. Apparently, she did not approve of the familiarity of her son's name on my lips. When I didn't immediately tuck tail and leave, she inhaled through her nose. "You should come back at a later time. He's in a volatile mood."

I shifted my weight from foot to foot before forcing myself to stand still. "I really need to see him now. Can you tell him Riley is here?"

At the mention of my name, recognition flashed in Irina's eyes, and her lips turned down as she stared at my Nirvana shirt. "You should come back another time," she repeated, this time with more frost in her voice. "When he gets like this, he's not fit for company."

Before she could close the door in my face, I lifted my chin. "I'll take my chances."

Irina studied me for a long, uncomfortable minute before opening the door and stepping aside. "Very well." She gestured toward the back of the house. "He's in there. I would walk you, but my presence will only make it worse. I trust you know the way?" Her voice was resigned, a note of pain buried deep beneath the civility.

"I do."

I followed the haunting music to one of the few rooms in Volkov's house I'd never been in. As I reached the arched entry to a formal sitting room, there was a lull, and then the tentative notes of a new song rang out. I stopped in the entryway, watching the man playing them. Max Volkov sat at a black Steinway grand piano. The song began softly, and it was familiar, even though I couldn't name it.

Seated at that piano, he looked nothing like the buttoned-up businessman I was accustomed to nor the alpha who controlled his world with an iron will. He was shirtless, in dark jeans and bare feet, his hair messy. His gaze focused on something I couldn't see as he coaxed the music from the piano. The sight of Vokov's big body curled over the keyboard —the play of muscle in concert with the music—hit me right in the ovaries. He was unraveled in a way I'd never seen him, and I felt the glide of his fingers over the ivory keys as surely as if he were touching me.

He closed his eyes and stilled, his fingers hovering above

the keys for several heartbeats. I held my breath. And when he began to play again, the tempo quickened, the music uplifting despite his tortured expression. He was lost to it, oblivious to me standing here, watching him because I couldn't look away.

Every note landed in my chest, every shift in tempo tangling my emotions. His fingers danced masterfully over those keys, and he bore a twisted mix of joy and despair on his beautiful face. As the music reached the crescendo, I closed my eyes and let it lift my spirit, and when it bottomed out, I didn't try to battle back the tears. Just when I thought it might end, it swelled again, carrying me with it.

When it was over, I opened my eyes to clash with his stormy gaze. He blinked, but still, he didn't speak.

"Max," I whispered, taking the first step closer to him. "You have a gift."

His jaw tightened, and his fingers dropped into his lap as he watched me cross the room.

"What was that you were playing?" I asked softly, the question doing nothing to break the tension stifling the room. When I'd first met this man, he'd taken up so much space, his presence filling every gap until I had no choice but to feel him. I'd been afraid of it then, but today, I moved in until I stood at his side.

Volkov was quiet so long, I didn't think he'd answer me. Finally, he spoke, his voice thick with an anger I couldn't reconcile with that song still lingering in my head. "Tchaikovsky's Waltz of the Flowers."

I searched for a description that would do it justice. "It's breathtaking," I said at last.

He nodded. "It was Anya's favorite song."

With her name, the emotions clicked into place. Music had always been my escape, my lifeline, so I understood the dichotomy of joy and grief wrapped in a single song. I didn't push for more, but I waited in the hope that he'd share it.

Volkov held out a hand, and I took it. He pushed back from the piano and settled me sideways on his lap, our eyes catching and holding. "It's from The Nutcracker," he said. "That was her dream—to be a prima ballerina one day, dancing on stage with the Bolshoi Ballet. Dancing was Anya's great love." Tears filled his eyes, and he blinked them away, rage taking their place. His arm tightened on my waist. "She should have had the chance to experience it."

I turned my head, dropping a kiss to his bare chest. "I'm so sorry she was cheated of that, and I'm sorry you were cheated of time with her." His heartbeat raced beneath my cheek, so I changed the subject. "I didn't know you were so musically talented. How long have you played?"

His hold eased. "Since I was four. I used to love it the way she loved to dance, but I rarely play anymore."

He didn't have to say it was because it reminded him of his sister, but I knew that to be true. I needed to lighten the grief that weighed him down, so I turned the conversation to lighter fare. "With that kind of musical ear, it must have been excruciating for you listening to me sing karaoke."

A laugh rumbled through him before he caught himself, and he gazed down at me. "You know you can't sing?"

I laughed. "Of course, I know I can't sing. I have ears."

Volkov shook his head, a hint of a smile on his full lips. "But you do it, anyway?"

"You don't have to be good at something to love it, Max. Love and pride are not the same thing."

"No. They're not." His voice faltered, but his gaze held steady. Then he lowered his head and kissed me with all the intensity he put into that song—alternating soft and sweet with hard and demanding.

I twisted on his lap, winding my arms around his neck and pressing my body to his. Everywhere we touched kindled like a flame. Nothing mattered beyond the feel of bare skin against mine, the scent of cedarwood cocooning me, and the taste of him when he teased my tongue. Volkov stood with me in his arms and walked us toward the door.

He stopped abruptly, his whole body going rigid, when Irina entered the room. She carried a tray of crackers, fruit, and cheese in her hands, open disapproval on her face. Volkov set me back on my feet and took a deep breath. I watched the change, turning him from raw, disheveled man into tightly controlled alpha, and I hated it. He didn't meet my eyes.

"Mother."

Irina sat the tray on a side table. "I thought you might like refreshments while you discussed whatever business brought your guest here."

I expected him to deny that business had anything to do with us, but he didn't contradict her. And he didn't introduce us.

I cleared my throat. "How thoughtful of you."

"No need," Volkov cut in. "I was about to drive her home."

Her. The word was so close to kid and girl, that I couldn't stop my hands from clenching into fists.

Volkov noticed. "Riley," he corrected. "I'm taking Riley home."

Irina stared at his half-dressed state and then swept her gaze to me.

"Let me grab a shirt, and we can go." He seemed hesitant to leave us alone, but after sending his mother a warning look, he left to get dressed.

Irina watched him go before turning to me. "Why don't you come over for lunch tomorrow?" Her smile seemed strained. "Just the two of us."

I blinked, not quite sure what to make of her sudden invitation. "Max won't be here?"

"My son will be busy with his little charity event." She frowned as if she welcomed his charity work about as much as she'd welcomed me. "This time of year, he's always busy."

"And you want to have lunch with me?" I should say no. If Volkov wanted his mother to get to know me, he would've introduced us when he had the chance. But I was curious. "Why?"

"There are things you should be aware of, things my son should have shared."

My pulse kicked up, and my imagination ran wild. Before I could dig deeper, Volkov's bedroom door closed, and the sound of his footsteps echoed down the hall.

"One o'clock," Irina said. She picked up the tray she'd brought and disappeared into the kitchen before I could answer.

When Volkov returned, he was back in a business suit, his expression locked down. "Shall we?"

I didn't move. "Max, are we okay?"

"Of course." When I still didn't budge, he sighed. "Riley, everything is fine. With my mother, it's complicated, that's all."

"Complicated how?" I pushed. *Was he embarrassed of me?* I doubted I fit the mold of the women he normally dated, even when I wasn't dressed in loungewear.

He ignored my question. "You can tell me what brought you here on the drive." His phone rang, and he seemed grateful for the interruption. "Yeah?" He stepped out of the room, so I could only hear his side of the conversation. His expression darkened. "You sure you want to play that card with me?" Volkov clenched his jaw as he listened to the response. "Fine. One hour."

Volkov hung up and stared at me. "That was Celeste. She's called an emergency Tribunal video meeting in an hour. The Kansas City coven has filed a complaint, demanding you surrender yourself into their custody to continue the evaluation they started." His eyes flashed amber. "That's why you're here?"

I nodded.

Volkov glanced toward the kitchen where his mother was putting the food back into the refrigerator. "For privacy, I'd like to meet at your headquarters if you have no objection. My mother tends to get involved where she's not needed."

"That's fine. I'll text Kali, so she knows." Thankfully, Kali served as the Tribunal's representative for the necromancers. If it came to a vote, I could count on hers.

"Good." Volkov grabbed his keys. "Let's get this over with."

CHAPTER 17

Helen, Bea, Alyce, and Janis showed up battle-ready. Helen had pulled out the black cardigan she reserved for funerals and hair dye days. Alyce came armed with snack food, Janis with headache tonic, and Bea with a Snitches Get Stitches t-shirt and big hair.

Kali got there fifteen minutes before the scheduled call. Dez, our resident tech support, was the last to arrive at headquarters a few minutes later. Although I could've easily set up the video call myself, the more friendly faces I surrounded myself with, the better.

"Hey Dez, thanks for coming."

He grabbed the bowl of popcorn Alyce brought, flipped on the monitor, and plopped on the couch. "Are you kidding me? I wouldn't miss this episode of the Great Witch Wars for anything."

Kali laughed and gave him a high five, not even pretending to be a neutral party, before sitting beside him. I dropped into the seat on the other side of Dez and grabbed a handful of popcorn. Rather than join us on the big comfy couch, Volkov remained standing for the call in a classic power play.

"Any luck narrowing our suspects yet?" I asked Dez. With almost two hundred to wade through, it wasn't a job I envied him.

"I haven't even made a dent in the list. So far, no one jumps out as a lead," he admitted. "We need a way to narrow the list, or this is going to take forever."

Kali tapped her lips and looked at Helen. "Is there a witch registry he could hack into to run the women's names through?"

I'd already brought Helen and the girls up to speed, so she knew which list Kali meant. "There is a central registry, but no information other than names are in it—no addresses or photos. The Witches' Council has been careful to minimize the chance of data leaks that could compromise the safety of our witches."

I thought about my recent intake evaluation with the coven. "What about medical records? I assume a physical is required for every new witch when they join a coven, right?"

"That's true," Helen said.

"Do the covens each use local labs to process the bloodwork, or is there a central lab?" I asked.

Helen shrugged. "That, I don't know."

Martha would know, as would Celeste, but I doubted either of them would respond well to the question. I should've thought of this earlier, so I could've snooped at coven headquarters before I escaped. There might not be an easy way to narrow the search for the witch, but there might be for my attacker. "What about the pool chemicals?" I asked. "Is there a way to check to see who bought pool chemicals in the area within the last month?"

Dez nodded. "Smart. It'll take a while, but it'll be quicker than going through the list one by one." Dez checked his watch. "It's time. Everyone ready?" At our nods, Dez connected the call.

We were the last to join. Thanks to the jumbo-sized flat screen, we could see everyone else clearly.

The Tribunal included four voting members, one representing each of the supernatural factions within the Interior Territory. Kali represented the necromancers and Volkov the shifters. Because the remaining two members—Celeste for the witches and some vamp I'd never met—did not reside in Kansas City, they only showed up for critical meetings in person. The rest they opted for video conferencing, like today. In addition to Celeste and the latest vampire representative, Martha was also on the call.

Volkov served as the head of the Tribunal, which meant calling emergency meetings like this one was normally at his discretion. Given his clenched jaw and flashing eyes, he wasn't happy about whatever Celeste threatened him with to force this meeting.

Volkov didn't give Celeste a chance to ease into it, going on the offensive. "Why the fuck are we here, Celeste?"

Martha huffed and straightened her mauve blazer.

"Is she wearing shoulder pads?" Kali asked out of the side of her mouth. "I'm all for vintage fashion, but that's a step too far."

I shrugged and reached for another handful of popcorn, ignoring the death glare Martha shot my way.

Celeste took Volkov's f-bomb in stride. Of course, she'd worked with him long enough to be desensitized. She was also far more politically savvy than Martha. With her off-the-shoulder peasant top, ready smile, and dark Havana twists pinned back, Celeste appeared far more easy-going than she was. She not only held a seat on the Tribunal, she also led the powerful Witches' Council, which served as the world-wide governing body for witches—an impressive feat for a woman who looked to be in her thirties.

Celeste wrote something on a sheet of paper and handed it to her assistant, who scurried off. "The Kansas City coven has requested the Tribunal's assistance to ensure a novice witch undergoes formal magical evaluation and classification," she said.

Helen muttered something under her breath, but Celeste continued.

"According to the high priestess," she told Volkov, "you have a conflict of interest in this matter because you are dating the witch in question." She looked between us with an arched brow.

Volkov crossed his arms over his chest. "No."

Martha sputtered. "He can't just say no."

Celeste held up a hand. "No, you're not dating, or no, you won't recuse yourself from the vote?"

"Stop wasting my time. I'm not stepping aside." Volkov glared at Martha. "You have ten minutes to make your case, then we'll vote and get this nonsense over with, so I can get back to work."

The logical part of my brain understood that acknowledging we were dating would only embolden Martha. But the interaction with Volkov's mother was still fresh, and his silence stung, nonetheless.

"The witch has a point," the vampire representative said. Norman was new to the Tribunal. Unlike the last two vampire representatives who had old-world snobbery down to an art form, Norman looked like a middle-aged neighbor who loved to mow.

"That's not how this works," Volkov said. "Every member of the Tribunal gets a vote so that all the factions have a voice in governance. Are you going to step aside every time a case involves a vampire you know? I didn't think so."

"Fine," Celeste said. With her position on the Witches' Council, she must know a precedent like that would mean she'd be abstaining from a lot of votes. "Martha, please proceed."

Martha sat up straighter. "Before we get to the evaluation, I wish to lodge a formal complaint."

Helen smiled. Alyce rubbed her hands together. Dez threw a handful of popcorn in his mouth and elbowed me in the side. The only one who didn't look happy about this development was Celeste.

"What is the complaint?" she asked.

"I want something done about those rogue witches." Martha pointed into the camera.

Bea traced the letters on her t-shirt with her finger and blew her a kiss. "You hear that, girls? We've gone rogue."

"You see what I'm dealing with?" Martha asked. "This is a serious matter. They've been wreaking havoc for a week. They are out of control."

Celeste sighed. "What exactly have they done?"

"What haven't they done? First, there were the cicadas."

Helen widened her eyes in mock innocence. "This time of year, they are a pain, but you should be grateful you don't live in Iowa."

Janis nodded, flipping her long henna-red braid over her shoulder before leaning closer like she was letting Martha in on a secret. "I saw on the news that they're getting hit with both thirteen-year and seventeen-year cicadas. First time they've emerged together in over two hundred years. Can you imagine the noise?"

Martha's nostrils flared. "That is not what I'm talking about. I know it was you who let them loose in our juice bar. And that's not even the worst of it." Martha's face flushed as she listed her grievances. "They put an illusion spell on coven headquarters that made it look like we were mooning passing cars."

Dez and I both snickered. I caught Bea's eye and mouthed "good one" because I was sure that had been her idea.

"Get to the point," Volkov snapped. "We're not here to talk about petty pranks."

"Pranks?" Martha's voice shot up an octave. "We had the human police show up and issue a citation for disorderly conduct. Twice. The first time was because those witches paid to have a vending machine installed in front of my door with obscene t-shirts in it."

"How can a shirt be obscene?" Helen scoffed.

Bea's eyes twinkled. "What did the shirts say?"

Martha didn't take the bait. "They need to be stopped. All I've got done this week is deal with their attacks."

Alyce slapped her knee and cackled. "Attacks. Honey, you haven't seen our attacks yet."

"What would you call it then?" Martha demanded. "The jaywalking ticket? The library fines?"

"The wine distributor dropping your Bunco night deliveries," Alyce added gleefully.

Martha looked like a bull who was about to charge. "You see! They admit it."

Helen crossed her arms over her thin chest and smiled. "It seems like you're getting into a lot of trouble with the law,

Martha. Maybe we should be talking about whether you're fit to lead the coven."

"You think you can fill my shoes, Helen?" Martha sneered.

"Not with those size ten feet of yours," Helen shot back.

Martha poked her finger aggressively at the camera. "I demand that something be done about those Stitch Witch bitches."

"Enough!" Volkov thundered. "Get to the point of this meeting, or those witches will be the least of your troubles."

Martha's eyes flared. "Are you threatening me, alpha?"

"Yes."

Celeste tried to wrangle everyone back on topic. "Your complaints are noted, Martha, but we're here for one reason only. You requested the Tribunal force Riley Cruz to submit to magical evaluation. Is that correct?"

"It is," she said stiffly.

"She's not part of your coven, Martha," Helen said.

"According to Article III, Section IV, she's subject to my authority." This time, Martha didn't pull out her pamphlet, reciting from memory. "As an unaffiliated witch living in the greater Kansas City area, Riley Cruz is subject to the jurisdiction of the Kansas City coven for evaluation and training."

"She's not unaffiliated. Riley is with us," Helen argued. "I'll train her."

"You?" Martha shook her head. "Last I checked, you're not part of a coven, Helen."

"She's right," Celeste agreed. "As an untrained novice, Riley must be under the supervision of a registered coven."

Although I'd enjoyed watching Helen and the girls deliver a smack down, I didn't like where this was headed. "Aren't you all forgetting I'm a shifter?" I asked.

Volkov nodded. "She's right. Magic or not, Riley is a shifter. That puts her under my jurisdiction, not the coven's."

I bristled at the idea of being under anyone's jurisdiction but held my tongue.

Celeste tilted her head. "Is she pack?"

I met Volkov's gaze, answering before he could. "I'm pack adjacent."

"What does that even mean?" Martha asked.

Bea winked at me. "That means she gets to see the alpha naked but doesn't have to follow any of his bullshit rules."

Celeste cut off the laughter with a raised hand. "Be that as it may, if she's not under Volkov's authority, she's subject to mine."

I pinched my leg to prevent me from telling her where she could shove her authority. Antagonizing a witch as powerful as Celeste wouldn't be wise, despite the temptation.

"Let's vote," Volkov said. "All in favor of granting Martha's request?"

Both Celeste and Norman voted aye.

"Against?" Volkov and Kali cast their votes. "As the head of the Tribunal, I cast the tie-breaking vote." Volkov looked directly into the camera. "No. Meeting adjourned."

"I'll take this to the Enclave if I have to," Celeste threatened.

Hopefully, the fact that I was hunting down dangerous demon artifacts for the Enclave would be enough reason for them to deny Celeste's request. Of course, as far as the Enclave knew, my magical abilities were as run-of-the-mill as any novice witch. They might not see any harm in forcing me under the coven's authority, and it wasn't like I could tell them about my null abilities. Demon artifacts or not, the Enclave would declare me a threat to be handled.

"You should be careful, Celeste," Volkov warned. "I'm not an enemy you want to make." He snatched the remote and killed the call. Then he turned on me. "You need to reconsider, so I can put an end to this."

I didn't have to ask to know what he meant. "Max, we've been through this. I'm not joining the pack." It might be the easiest way to get Martha off my back, but the tradeoff was too high.

He raked a hand through his hair and ground his teeth. "Not every pack is like Carl's."

"I know that, but the only difference between a pack like Carl's and one like yours is the man leading it."

There were no votes or shared governance in a pack. While a good alpha would listen to his pack's council, he didn't have to. There was no fail-safe, and I'd lived under the consequences of that system too many years to ever go back to it. As I watched Volkov clench and unclench his fists, I couldn't find the words to make him understand that my answer wasn't a rejection of him. That was the problem. As the alpha, Max Volkov saw himself and the pack as one and the same.

A muscle worked in his jaw. "Do you understand that if the Enclave demands you turn yourself over, there will be nothing I can do to stop it?"

I swallowed. "I do."

"If it comes to that, tell me you'll consider joining the pack —temporarily at least."

We both knew a move like that would not be temporary. Whether tomorrow or next year, Martha and—now—the Witches' Council would never stop trying to force me into their ranks. Helen and the girls were proof of that. They'd made their position clear. As far as they were concerned, magic was something to be contained and controlled. The pack wouldn't tolerate me joining in name only either. If Volkov treated me differently than the rest of his pack, it would weaken his leadership.

I reached for his hand. He must have read the answer on my face because he stalked out the door without waiting for my reply.

CHAPTER 18

Irina Volkov was the kind of beautiful that made people trip over themselves to be in her orbit. Unlike her dark-haired son, she had golden honey hair along with those familiar pale blue eyes that were hard to look away from. Even I edged closer.

Kali had dropped me off on Volkov's doorstep a few minutes ago, with the promise to return in an hour unless I sent a distress call earlier. Kali had offered to come with me for moral support, but a conversation with the mother of the man I cared about was something I needed to do alone.

Irina's perusal was more subtle than mine, but no less thorough. "Please, come in. I've heard so much about you." She spoke like a politician, and it was hard to discern whether what she heard about me was a good thing or bad.

I also couldn't say the same. Max rarely spoke of his parents. "It's nice to meet you, Ms. Volkov." I followed her through the house to the library.

She smiled at me, but it didn't quite reach those frosty blue eyes. "No need for such formalities. You may call me Irina."

This woman, with her perfect hair and sharp smile, intimidated me in a way Max never had. I held out my hand awkwardly. Hers was cool against my palm, and I cringed when I shook it a little too enthusiastically. I dropped her hand and stared at the scuffed toe of the second-hand flats that pinched my toes. *I should've worn nicer clothes.*

"Please." She pointed to the seating area where a silver tray laden with dainty sandwiches and fruit sat beside a crystal decanter on a side table. Irina waited until I was seated in one of Volkov's leather chairs to perch in the one across from me.

Although I'd been in Max's library dozens of times, next to Irina, I was hyperconscious of how out of place I was among the rich mahogany bookcases and expensive antique furniture.

She gestured toward the tray of food. "Would you care for refreshments?"

For once, I didn't have an appetite, my stomach twisted in knots. Because I didn't want to be rude, I chose a plump red strawberry and took a bite.

Irina took nothing for herself. "Maxim tells me the two of you have become quite close."

At the word close, I had a flashback to the sight of Max leaning over me in that utility closet in Santa Fe and choked on the strawberry. Eyes watering, I hit myself in the chest to force it the rest of the way down. "We have," I managed.

A hint of a smile graced her lips before Irina poured me a glass of water, but it was gone so quickly I was afraid I imagined it. "I was surprised. You see, Maxim has always avoided entanglements." The words landed like a warning.

I sat my empty glass on the table and sat up straighter. "He's had a lot on his plate, building this pack from rubble." When Max moved to Kansas City to enter the tournament that selected the new alpha, the local shifters had been in disarray. He'd fought hard to lead, and since he took the mantle at twenty-one, he'd rebuilt the pack strong enough that even the most opportunistic alphas like Carl steered clear.

Irina inclined her head. "Even as a child, Maxim was relentless when pursuing something he wanted."

Based on the way she was watching me now, I wasn't sure if she was still talking about this pack or me. Either way, I didn't know what to say to that, so I said nothing.

Her gaze caught on the jewel flower tattoo peeking out from beneath the hem of the skirt I'd worn. "I like you. You remind me of myself when I was younger."

I gawked at her like a baby bird with my mouth hanging open, trying to pick out anything that I might have in common with this stunning woman. "I do?" I stared down at my chipped galaxy blue nail polish before glancing at Irina's pristine French-manicure.

Her lips twitched as she studied my pink hair. "Underneath all that fluff, I suspect you have steel in your spine."

Of course, I did. Women without backbones didn't survive this world.

She crossed her long legs and leaned back against the chair, tilting her head to take me in. Her gaze paused on the tattoo on my wrist and the hue of my hair. "I'll be blunt, yes?"

I nodded despite the butterflies that took flight in my gut. No one prefaced good news by asking if they should be blunt. I tipped my chin and waited for the blow.

Irina didn't hold back. "You are not what Maxim needs." Her piercing blue eyes—so like her son's—pinned me in my seat. "He is meant for great things. A life bigger than all this." She swept her hand around the room. "My son is enamored with you, and because of that, he thinks this is more than it can be. Maxim is young and determined to prove himself, but when his father steps aside, he will take his rightful place. He was born to rule."

And I was born in a gutter, clawing my way out of it. She didn't say it, but we both knew it.

Men like Volkov didn't often walk away from a legacy. Tradition and family had a way of getting their hooks in them, despite any attempts to escape the ties. Irina might be right. He might leave me broken-hearted.

I'd risk it.

"If you were sure of that, you wouldn't be here warning me off though, would you?" I asked.

She smiled. "You're a smart girl. We have that in common, too."

I stiffened when Irina's smile hardened to ice.

"Do you care for my son?" she asked.

"I do."

"Then let him go. He cannot afford divided loyalties." When I opened my mouth to object, she held up an elegant hand. "You are not pack and—unless I'm mistaken—you never will be."

I didn't correct her because she was right. I would never be pack. Not again. Some promises you made to yourself were unbreakable. That was mine.

"Do not make him choose. Maxim is an alpha. It's in his blood. He needs a woman by his side who will support him without question. A woman who understands what will be expected of him." Irina softened her voice, but her expression remained hard. "That cannot be you."

This woman cut me to the quick, but she was his mother,

so I gentled my tone. "Like you did when you moved here with Max and Aleksei?"

Volkov told me that she moved them to the states after the death of his sister, Anya. I picked a dainty sandwich off the tray and took an aggressive bite to still my tongue before I said something I'd regret. Anya was too deep a wound to breach.

"You know nothing of that." Irina waved a dismissive hand. "They were children then. I sent Maxim back when he was old enough to learn to lead." She looked down her nose at me, watching me swallow the bite of sandwich I'd taken.

I grabbed a glass, poured ice water from the crystal decanter, and drank it. "That's where we are different, Irina."

She arched a brow.

I leaned forward, so we were eye-to-eye. "I would never send my child back to a man like that."

"What do you know of such choices?" she scoffed. "You are but a child yourself."

"I haven't been a child since an alpha burned my parents alive when I was twelve years old, so he could get his hands on me." My voice trembled with anger and grief, and I clenched my fists in my lap. "And do you know why he did it?"

Irina's composure slipped, a note of sympathy threading her voice despite the rigid way she held herself. "Why?"

"Because my parents would have moved heaven and hell to keep me safe from monsters like him. The only way to me was through them." Blood or not, both of my parents had loved me fiercely. A tear tracked down my cheek at what that love cost them—and what their loss cost me. I didn't bother to brush it away as I met and held her eyes. "You sent a seventeen-year-old boy to a man you knew to be cruel enough to destroy him. You are his mother," I bit out. "Your job was to protect him, not support his father without question." I took a shaky breath. "Maybe you didn't have parents who showed you how, but I did. So, no. You and I are not the same."

I walked out of that room with my head held high and my heart shredded. Because as misguided as Irina was, she got one thing right. If it came down to it, I would never make Max choose.

CHAPTER 19

There were only two things that could cheer me up after a meeting like that—barbecue or breaking and entering. I started with the barbecue. With a belly full of smoked brisket, I changed into the stash of burglary-appropriate clothing I kept at headquarters for days like this, leaving the top button of my pants undone.

While Martha was forced to wait for approval to bring me in, I went hunting in her domain. Breaking into the coven building that night proved easier than breaking out of it earlier had been. All it took was a putty knife and a low-traffic side street. My dark clothes, black ski mask, and quiet footwear allowed me to blend silently into the shadows. Thanks to our previous witch-napping of Gwendolyn Reynolds, I knew the building layout well enough to come in through a guest room window after making sure no one was in the room. I closed the window, leaving a gap should I need a hasty retreat.

Despite it being nearly midnight, at least two witches would be on site. Helen told me the coven witches rotated twenty-four-hour shifts, like firefighters, to handle magical emergencies and to host out-of-town witches visiting the area. I pressed my ear to the door long enough to ensure the hallway beyond it was empty before easing it open. Keeping my footsteps light and my pace cautious, I headed to the main office. My trusty lock-picking kit got me inside, and I locked the door behind me.

Rather than risk the overhead lights alerting a roaming witch, I pulled out a small flashlight to survey the room. Martha's office held the standard big boss desk and filing cabinets, a few potted plants, and a funky exercise ball chair I couldn't resist testing out. *Wildly uncomfortable but fun.* I made a mental note to add one to my headquarters' wish list before I got to work.

After sifting through the mail on Martha's desk, I rifled through the papers neatly stacked in a tray. They were mostly invoices, but none were for lab work. Several were for general office supplies. One invoice was for bulk fertilizer, another for an exterminator. I smiled thinking about Helen's cicadas swarming the juice bar and snapped a photo of the invoice with my phone to show her later.

Toward the bottom of the stack, I found a pamphlet for the coven's novice witch training program. Martha sure loved her pamphlets. Curious, I flipped through it. The first page was a PR-crafted pitch that made novice training sound like summer camp. Of course, the next page undermined that image with a curriculum list full of titles as riveting as an economics textbook. The bulk of the pamphlet was dedicated to the training progression. Their program spanned three years of skills acquisition, broken into neatly organized phases. Three years of rigid supervision and regular testing.

Oh, hell no. I slid the pamphlet back into the pile with a shudder.

Before I could bust into the filing cabinets, I heard voices outside the door. I searched the room for a decent hiding place, but without closets, there were no good options. I clicked off my flashlight and crammed myself in the only available hiding space, tucking my legs to my chest to make myself as small as possible. If I was busted huddling under Martha's desk, I'd never live it down. Plus, explaining how I bypassed the coven's extensive wards would be difficult. The door opened, and the overhead light turned on.

"Where does Martha keep the overnight kits?" The woman's voice was familiar, but it took a second to place it. *Alona.*

"Over there," a second woman's voice said.

I held my breath. *Please, don't let her be pointing at this desk.* If those overnight kits were stashed in the roomy bottom drawer, I was so screwed. When no one approached the desk, I exhaled.

"Do you know who the emergency intake is?" Alona asked.

"Martha said it was a child, an eleven-year-old girl," the other woman said. "Someone found her in an abandoned building, said she was half feral."

"She's not an animal. Poor girl was probably scared half to death." A chair scraped the floor as Alona must have grabbed the kit. "What about her parents?" she asked.

"No clue." The other woman's voice was further away, and from the sound of keys jangling, she must be grabbing them from the far wall as they talked. "Poor thing can't control her power."

"What kind of powers does a child have?" Alona sounded surprised. Witches typically didn't manifest powers until adolescence, which is why training rarely started earlier than the teens.

The other woman lowered her voice, despite it being the middle of the night with no one around. "They said she's an elemental but didn't specify what kind. Can you imagine being that young and trying to control that level of power? I wouldn't be surprised if she lit something on fire or flooded her school and then ran away scared that she'd get in trouble."

Footsteps moved toward the door. "We're putting her in the guest room alone?" Alona asked.

There was a pause. "No, she's going in the containment room. Without control, she'll be unpredictable and potentially dangerous. Martha wants her isolated until transport arrives."

Alona sighed heavily. "That's awful though. She must be so scared."

"We'll grab her a stuffed animal and put on cartoons. It's only for one night."

"How long until she arrives?" Alona asked.

"Thirty minutes or so."

The door clicked closed behind them, but I stayed curled in a ball for several minutes, thinking about that young girl wrestling with a power she didn't understand. I couldn't imagine how terrifying that must be. As much as I resented the coven's interference in my own life, I was happy they were here to provide shelter and safety to this child until her parents could be located. I wondered what my life would have been like if anyone other than Carl had taken me in.

I set a timer on my phone for fifteen minutes, stretched my legs, and then resumed my search. The filing cabinets were locked, but Martha stored the key in her top desk drawer. The first cabinet held general files. I pulled out a file labeled Containment & Rehabilitation Protocol, curious what that meant for the child about to arrive. The file was several pages long and contained risk assessment categories that were color coded.

Pale yellow indicated someone of unknown risk and outlined procedures and a timeline for monitoring and assessing the witch. The standard observation time was listed as twenty-four hours. At the other extreme was code red, which was described as someone posing imminent danger to the supernatural community. The protocol for handling such a person included full body magic-canceling restraints, solitary confinement, and round-the-clock monitoring. The time frame for code red was indefinite.

Sweat beaded on the back of my neck when I considered where they'd likely place me on that continuum should they discover I was a null. Somehow, I didn't think they'd code me yellow. I put the folder back and checked the time. Five minutes. The remaining filing cabinets were organized alphabetically by last name. I opened the A-C cabinet and located the folder with my name on it.

Surprisingly, there were already several papers in it. My recent physical was on top. I scanned the pages until I found what I was looking for. *Bingo.* The lab address wasn't local. After sending a photo of the lab name and address to Dez, so he could hack into their medical records and hopefully find a match for our hex witch, I flipped through the remaining pages. One of them was a general bio with known associates, listing Helen and the girls. But it was the last page that made me nervous. It flagged several incidents as worthy of monitoring, along with notes for each. I ignored the entry for petty theft when I was sixteen and focused on the last two entries.

One was an account of an altercation with the Kansas City alpha at Grinders. The barista noted that I was intoxicated and hyped up on coffee beans. I cringed. *Not my finest hour.* But what concerned me was the notation about an alpha command that affected everyone else on the premises but seemed to have no effect on me.

The second was Gwendolyn Reynold's description of what happened the day Volkov and I questioned her outside her apartment. Like the barista, she noted that when Volkov commanded her to stop, it affected her but didn't affect me.

"Shit," I muttered under my breath. This was not good. I might not be wearing a null nametag, but this was abnormal enough to snag the coven's interest. How long would it be before Martha or Celeste connected my immunity to alpha commands to a general immunity to magic? And, more importantly, what would they do to me when they found out what I was?

CHAPTER 20

No one had a better eye for design or an appreciation for a good bargain than Kali, which is why she was my plus one to the kitchen aisle at Home Depot the next afternoon. We'd set up our home improvement inspiration date last week to look at countertops and bar sinks. With everything going on, I'd forgotten all about it until she'd knocked on my apartment door thirty minutes ago. I was happy for the distraction.

"What do you think of this one?" I held up a mid-priced laminate countertop sample.

Kali snatched it out of my hand. "No." She pulled me over to the section with granite and quartz samples. "You, my friend, have earned real stone. Check these out." She pointed to a row on sale this week.

After staring at the samples for a good five minutes, I gave up. "I don't know. There are too many choices."

Kali snorted. "There are never enough choices. Are you going for industrial chic or cottage core?"

"Huh?"

"What do you want for your headquarters?"

I perked up. "Definitely a climbing wall, maybe a ping-pong table. Oh, and I want one of those heated toilet seats, but it doesn't have to play music."

She laughed. "No. I mean style-wise, what do you want?"

I shrugged. "That's why you're here."

Kali shook her head and picked out two samples, holding them up. "This travertine would be fun with all the old wood in the warehouse, or you could go classic with a granite like this one."

"Let's take them both." I grabbed the samples out of her hands and shoved them in my pocket.

"Speaking of style." She stared at my preppy outfit and uncomfortable shoes. "Why are you dressed like an Easter egg?"

I blew out a breath. "Because Irina Volkov got in my head."

"You're fabulous as you are. If she doesn't see that, she's missing out." Kali flicked the collar of my robin egg blue polo. "And this shirt is the most hideous thing I've ever seen."

"Bea gave it to me as a gag gift one year for my birthday." I grimaced. "I really hate it."

"See? You do have some style sense." She linked her arm through mine. "Let's put it to good use in the next aisle."

We picked out a couple sink options for the bar, and I took photos with my phone. Kali planned to make a design collage like those on home improvement shows to show the team. I was positive Dez and Nash would have zero opinion on renovation finishes, but I didn't want to spoil her enthusiasm.

My phone rang as we were leaving the store. "Hey Bea, what's up?"

"I brought another load of magical texts over this afternoon, and good thing too, because you have a visitor." She lowered her voice. "And he's a hottie."

I'd made spare keys for the whole team, so they could come and go from headquarters as they pleased. So far, Bea was the only one who had used hers.

"Volkov?" I guessed.

Bea chuckled. "No, but the alpha is a fine specimen as well."

At Kali's inquisitive look, I covered the phone. "Someone stopped by headquarters," I told her. If it wasn't Volkov, I had no idea who would drop by unannounced.

"What did you say your name was, sugar?" Bea asked someone in the background. "Says his name is Kage." She made a purring sound. "That sounds like a stage name, if you know what I mean."

I bit back a laugh. The Enclave's messenger was certainly attractive, but I highly doubted he'd ever worked as a male stripper. "Can you put him on the phone, Bea?" It was probably best if I didn't let Bea relay any messages. She had a way of making the most innocuous things sound downright dirty.

"Sure, hon." She put the phone on speaker.

"How soon can you be here?" Kage for Sato asked without preamble.

"What's this about?" I had a pretty good idea why he was here, but I wanted confirmation.

"It's best discussed in person," he said.

My nerves kicked in. That sounded a lot like something you'd tell someone you didn't want to bolt. I didn't feel like dancing around the issue, so I got straight to the point. "Are you going to take me into custody?"

"I'm not a cop," Sato said, which wasn't really an answer. When I remained quiet, he sighed. "I have additional information pertinent to the job you're working on. And we need to discuss the coven's request. Now, how soon can you be here?"

"An hour." When he balked, I pushed back. "If you wanted a fixed meeting time, you could have given me a heads up that you were coming."

"This wasn't a planned stop, Ms. Cruz. I'm on my way to handle another matter and thought this discussion would be best in person, so I made a detour."

That didn't sound like he was here to take me in. I relaxed a little. "I need to gather my team. An hour is the best I can do." If it were an emergency, he wouldn't be giving me the option of setting the time.

"Fine. One hour," Sato agreed.

"Don't worry, hon. I'll keep Kage company while he waits," Bea promised.

Sato didn't argue. Of course, he didn't know Bea either. By the time we got there, they'd either be best friends, or he'd be scandalized. Probably both.

I shot off a text to the group chat with the details and asked Kali to drop me off at headquarters rather than my apartment. Kali and Craig were flying to Chicago to visit her family in the morning, which would hopefully go better than their previous visits. She needed to spend the rest of the day packing and finishing some custom orders rather than sitting in a meeting, but I filled her in anyway.

Nash and Dez responded to my text right away, and Helen replied a minute later. When there was no response from Volkov, I dialed his number. No answer. That wasn't like him. I left a voicemail as we got in Kali's car. After five minutes without a call back, I dialed Teagan, the pack beta. She answered on the second ring. "

"Hi Teagan. It's Riley."

"Is everything okay?" she asked. The only other time I'd called Teagan was when Volkov had been shot, so it was a fair question.

"Everything's fine. I'm trying to get ahold of Max though, and he's not picking up."

There was a pause. "He's in a meeting," she said finally.

I tilted my head to hold the phone against my shoulder while I grabbed a receipt and a pen. "I need to reach him, Teagan. It's important. Where is the meeting?" I hoped it was close enough to drop by in person. He'd definitely want to be there for Sato's message, and I wanted the backup.

Teagan sighed and, after another pause, rattled off an address. Thankfully, it wasn't far out of our way. "He's organizing a charity event, so he'll be at the venue all afternoon," Teagan said. "He usually turns off his phone, so it doesn't disturb rehearsal."

I was curious what kind of charity event had him attending rehearsals regularly enough to have a known habit of shutting off his phone. Since she seemed hesitant to discuss it and I'd see for myself soon enough, I thanked Teagan and hung up.

When we arrived, I expected a high society fundraising event, so the stage full of preteen ballerinas took me by surprise. Kali and I gawked at the chaos as we stood in the back of the theater. At least a dozen girls in practice leotards huddled on stage. Two women distributed elaborate costumes amongst the dancers, while several moms chatted with one another in the audience seats. Volkov stood off to one side of the stage with his back to us, talking to a willowy woman with a neat bun and the legs of a lifelong dancer. Whatever they were discussing had her head nodding and her gaze darting anywhere but on Volkov.

Kali leaned close, her mouth hanging open. "What is happening?"

When the women on stage pulled out the flower costumes, my heart stuttered. "He's sponsoring a production of The Nutcracker."

Kali craned her neck. "Why?"

"Long story," I whispered before heading to the front.

"I wouldn't interrupt them if I were you," one of the moms near the aisle warned before I got far. "Mr. Volkov can be," she searched for an appropriate descriptor, "intense. Best to wait until they're done to talk to Daniella." The three women sitting with her nodded.

"I'm actually here to see Mr. Volkov," I said.

The women exchanged glances while checking out my pink hair. The woman who warned me elbowed the others when they stared too long and cleared her throat. "It's just wonderful what he's done for the girls." She pointed at the stage and then at the plush seats around us. "Paying for this rehearsal space and funding all the costumes for the production. My daughter is over-the-moon about her costume. It's absolutely gorgeous, far nicer than anything we could have afforded."

"He paid for everything?" Kali asked.

"Oh yes," a woman with a sharp nose and wispy brown hair said. "He's very involved."

"A bit too involved if you ask me," the third woman muttered, her full lips pressed into a thin line.

I cocked my head to the side. "What do you mean?"

The other two women flared their eyes in warning, but the disgruntled mom wouldn't be silenced. "Just that it's unusual for someone without a proper dance background to be the one to select the lead in a ballet, but Mr. Volkov insists on doing so every year." She touched her hand to her chest. "My daughter is quite talented, you see, and—" The others glared at her until she trailed off. "Of course, we all appreciate his generosity," she added, her tone saying something else entirely.

"Of course," Kali agreed, even as she poked me in the side.

I watched a little girl try on a daisy costume, beaming at the woman who helped her into it. "When's the big performance?" I asked.

"The first performance is next week," one of the women said.

The overlooked star dancer's mom huffed. "It's a strange choice to perform The Nutcracker in the fall like this instead of the Christmas season."

"As a CEO, I'm sure Mr. Volkov is a busy man," the more diplomatic of the moms said. "Since he always attends the performances, this might be the only time of year that works for his schedule."

At that moment, Volkov turned and caught sight of us, effectively killing the conversation. He said something to the woman on stage and then headed our way.

He scanned my body, as if searching for injuries. When he found none, he frowned at my pastel polo and dress pants. "What's wrong?"

"I'm fine, Max." I put some distance between us and the gossiping dance moms, and he followed. "Sato showed up unexpectedly at headquarters. We're headed there now, and I thought you'd want to come. You didn't answer your phone, so I called Teagan. She told me where to find you," I explained.

Volkov didn't look happy at her disclosure, but he moved toward the exit without complaint. When we were in the parking lot, he pulled out his phone and turned the ringer back on. Kali looked at him like she was about to ask questions, but he cut her off.

"I'll meet you there in twenty minutes," he said, already walking to his car.

Kali waited until we were both sitting inside her lemon-yellow Volkswagen beetle to comment. "Wow. I knew Volkov was a control freak, but personally selecting the twelve-year-old lead for a kid's dance recital? That's next level micro-managing right there."

I watched his taillights disappear from view and swallowed past the lump in my throat because I understood why Volkov had to be the one to pick the lead. He wanted someone worthy of his sister's memory dancing across that stage, the haunting notes of her favorite song surrounding him. "He has good reason to be selective." I didn't elaborate because the reasons weren't mine to share.

CHAPTER 21

Somehow, Bea coaxed one of the deadliest men on the planet into playing a game of Twister to pass the time. We arrived to tangled limbs and booming laughs. Volkov stared as Bea and Sato collapsed in a heap on the large plastic game mat while Helen and Dez yelled encouragement from the couch. Rather than simply standing up like most people would, Kage Sato rolled back, kicking his legs high before they landed under his hips, and he jumped gracefully to his feet. He offered Bea a hand, his expression once again unreadable as if the two of them hadn't just been belly laughing like little kids.

Volkov regained his composure and faced Sato. "Tell me the Enclave is going to stay out of this."

"For now," Sato conceded. "We'll get to the coven request in a minute. First, we must discuss a development that affects the current job."

"We need to wait for Nash," I insisted. As impatient as I was, I wanted everyone here for this conversation.

Helen waved her phone in the air. "I've got him on a video call."

"Good." I joined her and Dez on the couch.

Both Sato and Volkov remained standing. Now that we were focused on business rather than Twister, Bea said her goodbyes including pulling Sato in for a full-body hug before leaving to help Alyce with an afternoon quilting demonstration.

I turned sideways, so I was facing the men, preoccupied with the threat of the coven hanging over me. I pulled out a stick of my cinnamon gum to settle my nerves.

"What's the development?" I asked.

"We have reason to believe that the demon spell book poses an even bigger threat than we knew," Sato said. "It's urgent that you find and secure that book." Because I'd already filled him in on our progress, he knew about the pair who snatched the book before I could.

Volkov tensed, his gaze locking on me. "What kind of threat?"

"We believe that book contains a ritual that could create an opening between realms," Sato said.

"Like a portal?" Dez asked, pushing his dark-rimmed glasses up his nose.

"More like a tear in the veil between the human world and the demon realm," Sato corrected.

That sounded worse. A portal could be closed. "And all someone needs to create the tear is that spell book?" I asked.

"No." Sato weighed his next words before speaking. "However, we can't know how many of the other components they have already acquired. Have you located the book?"

I looked at Dez. "Any progress narrowing the field?"

He nodded. "Yeah. I cross-referenced the pool chemical

purchases with our list and narrowed it to four likely suspects. I'm still working on the witch."

"Great work, Dez." Four was a huge improvement from seventy-six. "We can go over the suspects when we finish here." I turned to Sato. "Now, tell me what the Enclave is going to do about the coven's request."

Sato inclined his head. "Because you are working on a high priority case for the Enclave, they will not get involved until the spell book has been secured."

Volkov's eyes bled amber, his wolf rising to the threat left unsaid.

"And then?" I pushed.

Sato met my eyes. "Then they will probably rule in favor of the coven's request. However, until this job is over, you are not subject to evaluation. I've informed Celeste that unless you pose an imminent threat, you are free of her jurisdiction until the Enclave decrees otherwise."

My palms grew clammy at the temporary reprieve, recalling the coven's containment protocol and wondering where I'd land on the risk scale given their notes about my resistance to alpha commands.

Helen cocked a hand on her hip and glared at Sato. "You expect her to chase down your artifact despite those cowards not having her back?"

"I expect Ms. Cruz to do the job she signed on for," he said. "It's not like the witches are going to throw her in a dungeon. They merely want to evaluate her newly manifested magic. It's a valid request."

Volkov loomed over the man, barely holding himself in check. "Not if she's pack." He wouldn't look at me.

Staring at his stubborn face, annoyance and warmth rose in equal measure. Although frustrated with Volkov's continued insistence that joining his pack was in my best interest, I couldn't help the flutter of gratitude at the attempt to shield me. It was nice to know that whatever strain his mother had introduced into our relationship, this man would never stop fighting to keep me safe.

To his credit, Sato didn't flinch despite an angry werewolf crowding into his personal space. "She's not pack though, is she? And before you suggest it, the Enclave would not acknowledge your jurisdiction if she joined after the coven lodged their request. They'd see it as what it is—a blatant attempt to undermine the witches' claim and the Enclave's authority. The only reason the Enclave hasn't already ruled in the coven's favor is because getting that demon artifact is their highest priority."

Volkov stiffened. It might not have been what he wanted to hear, but at least it put that argument to rest.

Dez leaned back against the couch cushions, his cheeks ruddy and his eyes red with bloodlust. "On second thought, maybe I haven't narrowed down our pool of suspects. It might take a while."

"Months even," Nash threatened.

Both Helen and Volkov relaxed a fraction, but my muscles remained knotted. There was no way I could leave a book that dangerous in the hands of someone willing to use it for months.

Sato's neutral façade cracked, worry lines edging his forehead. "You don't understand. With the high demon king gone, the remaining kings are battling for dominion over their world and this one." He glanced at Dez, the frown lines growing deeper. "You can bet they're sending demons loyal to them every time a vampire is created."

The red in Dez's eyes receded, and he shivered. "They'll go after the book," he guessed.

"If they haven't already," I added.

Sato nodded. "According to the prophecy, if they get their hands on the spell book and the air and water elemental they'll be hunting, we won't be able to stop them. This is bigger than all of us."

"Who are these elementals?" Helen demanded.

Sato's answer was his standard company line. "I'm not at liberty to disclose that."

"And the prophecy?" Volkov asked.

"I'm afraid I can't share that either," Sato said. "The only thing I can tell you is that if you fail, there will be nothing standing in the way of a demon uprising unlike anything this world has ever seen."

When he put it like that, my coven problems didn't seem so big. Sato left with a promise that he'd give us warning if the Enclave ruled in the coven's favor once this was over. I had no idea what good such a warning would be, since there was nowhere on earth I could hide from the Enclave's reach, but at least I'd see the restraints coming.

Volkov dropped a quick kiss on my lips before leaving to handle pack business. Things might still be strained between us, but the kiss gave me hope we'd work out whatever the issue was once this threat passed. Because Dez still looked like he was about to tap a vein, I mixed him a blood-spiked Bloody Mary and passed out bottles of pop for the rest of us. Then my team got to work.

"Run us through your suspects," I told Dez. "We'll see if any of them stand out."

Dez grabbed his laptop from the coffee table and turned on the flat screen, projecting four photos with names under them. He pointed to the one on the top left, a balding man in his early fifties. "We've got one in Nevada, and another in Atlanta." He moved clockwise, pointing first to a gaunt man with a crooked nose—probably not our guy—and then to an average looking man with a crew cut and a stubborn jaw. "The one on the bottom left lives in Galveston, Texas." Dez indicated the last man, who was the least remarkable out of all of them. He was the kind of man who blended seamlessly into the background. "This guy is practically living in our backyard if his last known address in rural Nebraska is correct."

I sat up straighter and studied the last photo. Dark hair, proportionate features, and wary eyes. He could definitely be our man.

"Isn't all of Nebraska rural?" Nash's voice challenged from Helen's phone.

"Fair," Dez conceded. "I'll do some more digging and try to verify the addresses on their driver's licenses. Most states only require renewals every four to six years, so they could easily be out of date."

"Helen, can you flip the camera around, so I can see the suspects, too?" Nash interrupted.

"Oh, right. Sorry!" Helen turned her phone and aimed it at the flat screen mounted on the wall. "How's that?"

"Better," Nash said. "Zoom in on the bottom left suspect."

Dez did as he asked. Up close, the man had fine lines around his mouth and on his forehead, but there were no laugh lines visible. He wasn't a friendly sort, then.

"That's our guy," Nash announced. "I recognize him from the movie set. He was a set designer working on Corville's movie."

I stood and moved closer to the screen. "He does look familiar." I hadn't interacted with the man at all, but I'd seen him hanging around the set. I slapped myself on the forehead. "The witch wasn't there to see Corville. She was there because of this guy."

"What can you tell us about him?" Nash asked Dez.

"Not a lot yet, beyond his name and last known address," Dez admitted. "His name is Robert Thompson and, according to his driver's license, he lives about an hour west of Omaha. He's forty-six years old, five foot eleven, and a hundred-seventy-five pounds. It's not much to go on, but now that we know who to focus on, I'll do a deep dive. This time tomorrow, I'll be able to tell you where he lives, what he spends his money on, and when he got his last tetanus shot."

I clapped Dez on the back. "Awesome. Let's reconvene here tomorrow and plan the job."

"Are we going to talk about the elephant in the room?" Dez asked, looking between Helen and me. "What are you going to do about the coven?"

I had no idea. All I could do was tackle one threat at a time. "For now, let's focus on finding Thompson." Once we had the demon spell book out of circulation, I'd worry about Martha and her relentless rules. Until then, I had a job to do.

CHAPTER 22

As soon as everyone else was gone, Helen cornered me with hands on her hips. "Now explain to me why you're suddenly more worried about the coven than you were a few days ago."

When I told her about breaking into coven headquarters, Helen held up her hand for a high five. Her enthusiasm dimmed when I mentioned what was in my file and disappeared altogether when I described the containment protocols I read.

"I've never heard of that," Helen said. "Could you tell if it was from the Witches' Council?"

That was a good question. An official document handed down by the powers-that-be would carry a lot more weight than something Martha drafted up herself. I thought back to the documents in that file folder. "I don't think so. It looked like regular printer paper. I'd imagine if the Witches' Council distributed something like that, it'd be bound or on letterhead, right?"

"Right." Helen bustled around the room tidying up as we

talked. The fact that she was cleaning meant she was more nervous about the coven threat than she wanted to admit.

"Sounds like something Martha would cook up." Helen shook her head. "That woman is more afraid of magic than anyone I know."

"But she leads a coven. How can she be afraid of magic?"

"She may be the high priestess now, but I've known Martha since she was a novice witch trying to master basic spells. She's a natural leader, I'll give her that, but she didn't rise through the ranks because of any magical prowess. Martha is a middling witch who thinks magic is something to be controlled and bartered, like currency. Unless a witch is under her boot heel, she views anyone with real power as a threat."

"Well, since I don't have any power, I wish she'd leave me alone," I grumbled.

"Nonsense." Helen patted my cheek. "You have plenty of power."

I snorted.

Helen thumped me on the forehead.

"Ow!" I rubbed the spot. "What'd you do that for?"

"To knock some sense into that thick of head of yours." She grabbed a rag and wiped down the bar top.

I blew out a breath and risked another thump with a question. "How is my lack of magical ability power though?"

"Have you ever played with magnets?" Helen asked.

"Sure." I blinked at the abrupt change of subject.

"Flipped one way, they attract. Another and they repel." Helen grabbed a couple peanuts from the bar top to demonstrate. "Is the magnet any less powerful when it's not attracting?"

"Of course not," I said, understanding what she was getting

at. A witch typically attracted magic. The more powerful the witch, the more magic she could pull. Elementals were exceptionally powerful but attuned to a single element, while other witches could attract magic from multiple elements but not to the same magnitude. I might not be able to attract magic to use it, but that didn't mean I was powerless. "My null abilities are like a powerful repellent."

"Exactly." Helen grabbed a broom to sweep the area around the bar. "We already know that you can repel air-bound magic like commands and wards. Earth magic like potions also has no effect on you."

I thought back to the memory retrieval spell that Isaac performed with me. "But blood magic does."

Helen nodded. "That's not too surprising since blood magic is demon born rather than earth bound elemental magic."

"What about vampire compulsion though? Isn't that blood magic? Like alpha commands, compulsion doesn't affect me." I tried to puzzle how it might be different from something like the blood magic Isaac performed.

"That is curious," Helen agreed. "Maybe it's because the compulsion is spoken, thus drawing upon the air."

"Maybe." It was as good of an explanation as any I could think of. "What about the other types of elemental magic? Fire and water?" I tried to recall direct contact with either but couldn't dredge up any good examples.

Helen finally put the broom away and sat next to me on the couch. "We won't know unless we test it. What we need to do is figure out your limits."

I groaned because that sounded like a pitch for another magical gauntlet, this time with fireballs and waterboarding.

Helen patted my hand. "Don't be a baby."

"Fine. We'll test it." I turned my head to look at her. "But there better be cookies."

Her lips quirked. "I suppose I can arrange that."

My stomach growled on cue, and we both giggled. I grabbed a handful of peanuts to quiet the rumbling. "What happens after we uncover my limits?"

"Then you learn to embrace the power, Riley. You don't need Martha's b.s. three-year program to master your abilities. You have everything you need in here." Helen tapped my forehead, and then my chest. "And here. All you need to do is trust your instincts to guide you."

"When do we start?" I asked.

"No time like the present." Helen glanced at my outfit. "First, you better change out of those fancy clothes and put on sensible shoes. Things are going to get messy."

With Helen in charge, that was a given. I stood up and pulled Helen to her feet. "I left my spare burglary clothes at home after my coven break-in, so we'll have to swing by my apartment."

She grabbed her keys. "Let's go then. You can tell me why you're dressed like a middle-aged golfer on the way."

Helen wasn't wrong. How people wore clothes like this day in and day out was beyond me. From now on, I'd stick to my well-worn combat boots and comfy band tees. I followed her down the stairs and outside, locking the door behind me.

When we were in the station wagon, Helen pressed the issue. "Does this have something to do with whatever is going on between you and that alpha of yours?" Of course, she picked up on the tension. Helen knew me better than anyone. She started the car and pulled into oncoming traffic like a Nascar driver.

After years riding shotgun in Helen's station wagon, I

knew better than to grip what she referred to as the chicken handle, no matter how close she came to taking out another car while weaving in and out of traffic. I picked at my chipped nail polish instead. "Maybe."

Ever since I came to live with Helen as a teen, driving had been our bonding time, when Helen coaxed out my fears and worries. Today was no exception. After a few minutes, I told her about my lunch with Volkov's mother and her insistence that I was not the kind of woman her son needed.

Helen went full mama bear mode by the time I finished. "That woman should be thanking her lucky stars that you're giving that boy the time of day." She shook her head, muttering about people with silver spoons stuck up their butts.

"Is she wrong though?" I stared out the window. "Are we too different to make this work? Max keeps pushing for me to join the pack, but that's never going to happen. What if he can't let it go? Even if he can, what if she's right about him taking over his father's pack one day?"

Helen glanced at me before shaking her head. "Pack or not, he isn't about to give you up for power. I can tell you that much." Helen flipped her turn signal on mid-lane change and then flipped off the jacked up pickup driver who sped up to cut her off. "You didn't see him when you were missing. That man would burn down the world for you, hon—even if he is too bossy for his britches."

I laughed. "He is pretty bossy."

Helen parked in front of my building and shut off the engine. I leaned over the console and gave her a hug before we got out. We were halfway to my door when I realized I must have dropped my phone in the car.

"Be right back," I told her, jogging back to the car to get it.

Helen kept walking. She was almost to the building when I came up behind her and spotted the magical tripwire stretching across the threshold of the entryway door.

"Stop!" I screamed, breaking into a run when I saw it.

But I was too late. The explosion rocked me back on my heels, shattering windows and raining debris.

CHAPTER 23

I threw myself over Helen, wrapping my arms around her small body and tucking her head to my chest. Bits of brick and broken glass struck my back and legs as we lay motionless on the sidewalk. Panic overwhelmed me when Helen stilled, and I prayed I'd reached her in time. As a witch, Helen was such a powerhouse that it was easy to forget that she was also a woman in her seventies. A normal fall on concrete could easily break a bone or shatter a hip. Being mere steps from an explosion like this could cause significant injury.

When the debris stopped falling, I pushed myself to my knees and stared down at her prone body. Someone was yelling, but the ringing in my ears blotted out their words. I ignored everything but her, focusing on the woman who had been my anchor in this world since I landed in Kansas City as a teenage runaway. She looked so frail lying there with her eyes closed and her skin pale, gashes marring the weathered skin of her cheek.

Pressing my head to Helen's chest, I choked back the sobs

until I felt the flutter of her breath rising against my cheek. "Please be okay," I whispered, gathering Helen in my arms. I sat on the sidewalk surrounded by the remnants of my apartment building, her head cradled in the crook of my arm, and I bargained with the universe. I would do better. Be better. If only she was spared. She may have lived a full life, but I wasn't ready to lose her.

I brushed the dirt from her dove gray cardigan, knowing it was her favorite and searched desperately for the pulse in her wrist. When I found the steady beat, I kept my fingers pressed against it, vigilant for any stutter. It never faltered, and after a few tense moments, her eyes opened. Finally, I could breathe freely again, gulping in great lungfuls and rocking with her in my arms.

Helen blinked several times and shook her head as if to dispel the ringing. Her deep brown eyes focused on my face. "Did one of my potion bombs blow up again?"

"No," I whispered. "Someone blew up my apartment building." Someone with magic, which meant that explosion was no accident. A witch tried to kill me, and Helen was collateral damage. "Are you okay?"

"I'm a tough old broad," she assured me. "It'd take more than a bomb to take me out."

I tried to smile, but fear still lodged in my throat. I ran my hands over her torso and down her back. "Anything hurt?"

"Everything hurts, hon, but I'll live."

When she tried to push herself upright, I helped her sit on her own. I looked at the destruction where my run-down apartment building had been. The shell of the building was still intact, but the entire top floor that included my apartment was rubble.

Now that the ringing was receding, I heard the

approaching sirens. Firefighters arrived first, the police second, and the two ambulances full of paramedics close behind.

"You sure you're okay?" I asked Helen.

She nodded.

Before emergency personnel were close enough to stop me, I ran inside the wreckage. I picked my way through the crumbled brick and mangled metal railing, searching for magical residue. The magical tripwire I spotted before the explosion was fractured but visible. Now that the bomb had gone off, it no longer pulsed with power. I made my way further inside, climbing over a half wall and scanning the area. There was no sign of magic anywhere else.

A strong hand gripped my bicep and spun me around. "Miss, it's not safe. I need to get you out of here in case the building comes down." The firefighter's voice was tinny. I didn't fight the hands that lifted me. He carried me out of the rubble, handing me over to the paramedics now swarming the scene.

Once assured I was capable of walking, a paramedic escorted me to one of the ambulances with its back doors open. "I'm fine," I told her.

"We need to check you over to make sure," she said.

I didn't argue, but I did search the growing crowd for Helen. When I spotted her being lifted into an ambulance, her body strapped to a stretcher, I pivoted in her direction. "I need to check on her."

"Okay. We can do that," the paramedic agreed when I wouldn't be deterred.

Helen was fully alert and barking orders when I reached her. The paramedic attending her was a shifter I recognized from my days working as a bartender at The Sundowner.

“Is she hurt?” I demanded.

“That’s what we’re going to find out,” he promised.

“What’s your name?” I asked.

He had the big build of a shifter but kind eyes. “It’s Ian.”

“Do you know who this is?” I asked, pointing at Helen.

“Yes, ma’am.”

My hands shook as I reached out and squeezed Helen’s hand in both of mine. “I need you to make sure she’s okay. Stay with her and don’t let anyone you don’t know get close to her. Do you understand?”

I had no idea if the witch who set off the explosion was long gone or lurking in the background, but I wasn’t about to take any chances when it came to Helen’s safety. It was bad enough she’d been injured in a blast likely meant for me.

Ian nodded. “I’ll stay with her. They may want to keep her overnight for observation, but I’ll make sure she gets to the hospital safe and sound.”

“Thank you. Which hospital? I’ll have someone there to watch over her.”

He gave me the name of the hospital. Assured that Helen was in good hands, I texted Alyce, Janis, and Bea to let them know what was going on. I relayed the hospital information to them and asked Alyce and Bea to guard Helen. It would likely be awhile before I was cleared to leave, but Janis insisted on leaving immediately to pick me up. Although I could drive Helen’s station wagon in a pinch, I wasn’t in the right headspace to risk it. Besides, I still didn’t have my license, and this place was crawling with police.

After everything was settled, I let the other paramedic take my vitals. Once she was convinced I was fine, she cleared me and directed me to a police officer taking statements.

Ian caught me before I could leave. “It’s for you.” He

handed me his personal cell phone. He must have known who I was and called Volkov because his deep familiar voice greeted me. "Riley, tell me you're okay."

"I'm okay. Other than some minor cuts and bruises, I'm unhurt. Helen was with me, but I think she's okay, too. They're taking her for observation to be safe."

Volkov's exhale was shaky. "Good. I'm on the other side of Kansas City dealing with a pack issue. I'm sending someone to pick you up and take you to my place. I'll be there as soon as I can."

The thought of sitting in Irina Volkov's judgment when my emotions were still so raw was more than I could bear. I wanted my own space to process what just happened and what I nearly lost. "I appreciate that, Max, but Janis is already on her way. I think I'm going to crash at headquarters tonight." I wanted to be close in case Helen needed me, and Max's place was too far out of the way. Besides, from the way my body was stiffening up, I wasn't going to get much sleep tonight, anyway.

There was a long pause. "I don't think you should be alone," Volkov said.

My gaze caught on the ambulance holding Helen. I didn't want to be alone either. "Janis will stay with me for a while. I'll have her set wards around the perimeter."

"Are you sure?" he asked.

"Yes. I'll give you a call as soon as I know more."

Two hours later, I was wrapped in an oversized blanket staring at the warehouse wall when I heard a commotion downstairs. Because Janis had warded the property against intruders intending me harm, whoever was on the first floor was a friend armed with a key. I stood on the landing, my sore body protesting the idea of going up and down stairs. Even in the dim light of the stairwell, I could make out Volkov's glacial blue eyes.

"Hey. You didn't have to come all this way to check on me," I said.

"Yes. I did." He climbed the stairs two at a time, carrying a couple brand-new boxes.

I held the door for him. "What's that?"

"Air mattress." He sat the boxes down. One had a photo of smiling kids sitting on a velvet-topped air mattress. The other held a bicycle pump. Volkov rubbed his stubbled jaw, frowning down at them. "I hope you know how to inflate one of these things, or we'll be sleeping on the floor."

"We?" My breath hitched, warmth settling in my chest and easing the tension coiled inside me.

"We. Wherever you are is where I need to be." He pulled me into his arms, one of his hands cradling the back of my head. He held me the way I'd held Helen, syncing his breathing with mine until he was sure I would be okay.

CHAPTER 24

The mood at headquarters was somber the following afternoon as the team gathered to make sense of the attack and plot our next move. Volkov handed off pack duties to Teagan, so he could stick around to help. Kali offered to postpone her Chicago trip, but I convinced her to go. There was nothing she could do here, anyway.

Dez, Nash, and Bea arrived a few minutes ago with Helen, who was released from the hospital this morning with a prescription for muscle relaxants and a warning to take it easy. Despite the sling on her left arm, Helen scooped Garth up when Nash let him out of his cage, settling the rooster on her knee like a grandbaby. Even Garth was subdued. He nudged Helen's good hand until she petted his back feathers.

Until we figured out who targeted me, no one could relax. Every time I caught sight of the yellow bruise on Helen's cheek, rage welled up, and I had to remind myself that she was okay. Volkov had reached out to his contacts in the police and fire departments this morning to get information on yesterday's explosion. So far, they hadn't come through.

I wasn't in a waiting mood. "Alright, let's start with what we know." While Dez opened his laptop, I went old school, snagging a piece of chalk from the brand-new box on the bar before moving to my new giant chalkboard wall. After sketching a rough outline of a building, I marked the spot where the magical tripwire was with red chalk. "The magic was here."

"You're sure it was a tripwire and not a ward?" Helen asked.

I thought back to the pulsing malevolence it gave off. "This magic felt different from protective or warding magic."

"But it wasn't keyed to you," Bea said. "Helen set it off when she opened the door. If it could be triggered by anyone entering the building, how could the witch be sure you'd be the one to set it off?"

"I guess it's possible whoever set it wanted to send a warning rather than outright kill me." Unless the witch was close enough to activate the tripwire when I showed up, whoever set it couldn't be sure I'd be home when it went off.

"The warning theory fits. As close as Helen was to the blast, she survived," Volkov reasoned. His phone rang, interrupting whatever he was about to say next.

We waited for him to answer it. A few minutes later, he hung up, a dangerous look in his eyes.

"That was one of my people embedded in the police department," Volkov said. "Here's what they know. The explosion was caused by a homemade IED. They believe it was placed directly outside Riley's apartment door."

That confirmed I was the target. I glanced at Helen's sling, wishing I would have insisted she wait in the car.

"Any casualties?" Nash asked.

"Not so far," Volkov said. "Fortunately, the explosion

occurred during the day when most people were at work. Other than Helen and Riley, there were a couple people on the other side of the building who suffered minor scrapes and injuries. But the landlord's son was in the apartment directly below Riley's fixing a garbage disposal when the bomb went off. He's in critical condition."

Any other day, and the landlord's son would have been fine since it was rare for him to actually fix anything. Despite the guy being a jerk, I hoped he pulled through. No one deserved to die crushed beneath building rubble. I rubbed my temples, the throb of a headache starting.

"Too bad my apartment building isn't the kind that has security cameras." Most days, I counted myself lucky if I had running water and a window that didn't stick shut. The only security on the premises was the overpriced alarm system Volkov had installed after Nash broke into my apartment several months ago. I looked to Dez. "Are there any traffic cameras or doorbell cams in the vicinity that you could tap into?" Even a grainy image could lead us to the culprit.

"Not likely." Dez pulled up satellite images of my street. "All the traffic cameras are aimed at intersections. Your apartment building is mid-block, and there are no houses with a direct line of sight either." Dez adjusted his glasses while he considered the options. "I can run the nearest traffic cam footage to pull license plates, but you live on a pretty busy street. Unless we spotted a vehicle we recognized, it would take at least a week to sift through everyone."

"And that's if they didn't park down the block and come in on foot," Nash said.

Since that was a dead end, I circled back to the magic. "Okay. We know a witch is involved. We can start with witches who have a motive to attack me." I wrote the most obvious name on the chalkboard. "Our hex witch is definitely suspect number one."

"Add Zara Bellarose to that list," Volkov insisted with a snarl.

I wrote her name as well. Those were the obvious two, but I thought about who else might have reason to target me. "I'm not sure why the coven would stoop to blowing up my building, but we should consider them, too."

Helen and Bea looked like they wanted to object, but they didn't say anything as I wrote Martha's name below the others. No one could think of any other suspects, so we examined the three we had. Above their names, I added three columns, labeling them means, motive, and opportunity.

"Everyone on our list is capable of creating a magical tripwire, right?" I asked. At Helen's nod, I added checkmarks down the means column. "What about motive?"

"Taking out the competition gunning for the artifact seems like a good motive," Nash said. "The hex witch already tried to kill you once."

"True." I jotted down her potential motive before moving on to Bellarose. There was no question she was capable of doing something like this, but a motive was elusive. "What possible motivation would Zara Bellarose have to do this?" Although we kicked around a few possibilities, none of them seemed likely. I added a question mark in her motive column and moved on. "That brings us to Martha."

Helen sat Garth on the floor and scattered a handful of chicken treats she now regularly carried in her purse. She looked at the names on the chalkboard. "I don't like Martha, but I can't imagine her putting innocent people at risk like that."

I agreed with her, but we still needed to consider the

possibility. "She is the one with the most opportunity though since she's local. Maybe she didn't think anyone would be there during the day, or maybe she thought the explosion would be smaller."

"She could have easily put a tail on Riley to know she wasn't inside ," Nash added.

"What's the motive though?" Volkov stared at her name written in chalk. "Even if Martha suspected Riley was a null, all she needs to do is wait for the Enclave to order Riley to turn herself over. There's no reason to blow up her apartment."

"You're right," I agreed. "If this was a warning or an attempt to scare me, there's no way she'd think I'd turn to her for protection. Not with all of you around." I studied the chalkboard. "Maybe the who doesn't matter right now."

Everyone stared at me.

"Our priority is securing that demon spell book before someone uses it to put out a welcome sign for demons to overrun our world. I say we focus on the hex witch, since she's tied to our artifact thief. If she's the one who set off the bomb, we eliminate both problems."

Nash nodded, catching on to my rationale. "And if it's Bellarose or Martha, it'll be hard to target you when you're on the job rather than hanging out here."

"Exactly." I turned to Dez. "Can you get us up to speed on what you found out about Robert Thompson?"

Dez cleared his throat. "The most interesting bit I uncovered was his connection to our hex witch." He turned on the flat screen and projected a photo of the blonde witch. "Her name is Phoebe Thompson, and she's Robert's wife."

Volkov glared at Dez. "You could have fucking led with that."

I grabbed Volkov's hand and tugged him down to the couch with me to prevent him from strangling Dez.

Dez shoved his glasses up his nose and pulled up a satellite image of a modest ranch house with an overgrown yard. "This is the address listed on both Thompsons' driver's licenses. It's in a tiny speck of a town in south central Nebraska."

I leaned forward to study the house. "Any evidence they are there?"

"Yeah. There have been several credit card purchases in the area as recently as yesterday," Dez said.

Between the treed yard and the one-level layout with multiple entry points, breaking into a house like this would be easy. Too easy. "What's the catch?"

"The catch?" Nash asked.

"There's no way these two stole that artifact out from under me and are stupid enough to hide out in a basic rancher in the middle of nowhere with that spell book. It's too easy."

"You're right." Dez pulled up a second satellite image. "When I checked the property tax records, I found a second property listed under Robert Thompson's name."

I studied the photo that showed a concrete door and little else. "Is that some kind of tornado shelter?"

"So much worse," Nash said. "That is an old missile silo."

"From your enthusiasm, I take it that's bad," I said.

Nash hung his head. "Yeah. That's bad. Those things were built to keep nuclear missiles secure. Getting into one uninvited would be incredibly difficult."

For the first time since the explosion, my smile was genuine. "Challenge accepted."

CHAPTER 25

If the demon kings were recruiting, a prepper who spent his meager retirement savings to buy an old missile silo in the middle of nowhere Nebraska was a solid choice. According to Dez's sleuthing, Robert Thompson had an impressive stockpile of weapons and enough freeze-dried rations to survive a bona fide zombie apocalypse. Thompson's online footprint included frequent posts on prepper forums that abruptly stopped six months ago.

Our best guess was that it coincided with his vamp gotcha day. What we couldn't figure out was whether his witchy wife Phoebe summoned the demon inside him, or if he was using his newfound compulsion powers to control her. Either way, this job just got a lot more difficult.

"We know what kind of human weaponry they have at their disposal, but we also need to know how much supernatural firepower we'll be facing. Dez, what did you find out about our witch? Any idea how powerful she is?" I doubted the routine physical Dez dug up would tell us much, but hopefully he'd found something that would clue us in. "We know she's an air elemental because she used air magic to attack me. What else do we know?"

"Once I had a name and address for her, it was easy enough to hack into the local coven records. They actually used 1234 as their password." Dez slapped himself in the forehead and rolled his eyes. "It's a small coven, with members spanning four rural counties. Their records were sparse, and Phoebe doesn't appear in any of the monthly roll calls for the last six months," That tracked with the timeframe of her husband dropping off grid. "Phoebe was listed on a monthly meeting agenda last year though. She gave a demonstration about how to alter spells and rituals safely."

Great. An air elemental with a knack for adapting magic to suit her purposes was now armed with a dangerous book of demon spells.

We'd been at this for an hour when Nash voiced the question that had been nagging in the back of my mind. "Assuming she's our bomber, how did this witch find you? We all used aliases on set."

He was right. She would have no way of ferreting out our real identities. And it wasn't likely that she followed us to Kansas, not when her husband was the one with the artifact.

Dez coughed, looking sheepish. "I have a pretty good idea how she found you," he said. "While I was digging around in the lab records for Phoebe's identity, I checked out Riley's lab work to see if there was anything in it that we didn't want the coven to get their hands on."

"Good thinking." I should've thought of that myself "What did you find?"

"Not a thing. Your blood sample was logged in at the lab but never tested. It's listed as missing." When Volkov growled, Dez held up his hands. "I didn't think anything of it then. I figured it was damaged or misplaced, but now—" He watched Volkov warily. "I wonder if they could've stolen it to use in a blood-tracing spell."

Zara Bellarose certainly had access to that spell, but she'd have no reason to use it to locate me. She knew exactly where to find me. I supposed it was possible that the Thompsons worked for her, but that didn't ring true. If they'd nabbed the book for Bellarose, she'd already have the thing listed for auction. No need to come after me. Somehow, the Thompsons must have gotten their hands on that spell.

"Does everyone have a copy of this thing?" I asked. *Was I the only one too hesitant to use it?* The idea of using the spell to track down my blood relatives was tempting, but I'd resisted because of how volatile blood magic could be. My so-called powers were wacky enough without adding demon magic to the mix.

Volkov grimaced. "The spell Craig and Kali found was a copy."

I groaned. "Copied from the demon spell book."

"That's my guess. But I'm not convinced the Thompsons were the ones who tracked you down. Why go to all the trouble to find you?" Volkov asked. "They already had the book."

None of the pieces were fitting neatly together. We could be here all night puzzling it out. "Let's set the motive aside for now. We should concentrate on what the Thompsons are capable of throwing at us when we go after the spell book." I scooted close to Dez's laptop and stared at Robert Thompson's photo. "We have an idea what Phoebe is capable of, but Robert is a wild card."

The only bit of pertinent intel we had was our theory that he'd been turned into a vampire six months ago. However, that didn't necessarily make him a weak vampire. In fact, I'd lay money on him being a powerful one. Unlike the pop culture versions, vampires' power wasn't determined by age but rather by the strength of the demon housed in the human body. There was little chance that a six-month-old vampire with a weak demon inside him went after a coveted demon spell book. Whatever demon Thompson hosted came here with a mission to secure that book and, most likely, to use it to bring down the veil.

A chill skated down my spine when I considered how close he might be to accomplishing that mission. *Was Phoebe one of the elementals in the prophecy Sato mentioned?* "Sato said that the prophecy about ripping through the veil required a water and air elemental in addition to the spell book, right?"

Garth picked that moment to launch himself onto the coffee table, pacing back and forth like a feathered general. Since Helen was down to one arm thanks to her sling, I scooped him up and sat him on the floor again.

"Yes. He did," Bea said. "You think Phoebe could be the air elemental."

"I do."

"Even so, they'd still need a water elemental," Helen reasoned.

My stomach pitched when a new possibility hit me. *Unless it was one and the same.* I turned to Helen and Bea. "Have you ever heard of a witch with two elemental powers?"

Both women shook her heads. "Never," Helen said.

I relaxed. Elementals were rare, which meant it was unlikely they'd already found a water elemental willing to aid them. Back to the demon then, who posed the biggest threat. "If only we knew which demon Thompson hosted, we'd have a better idea what kind of power to expect."

Dez fumbled his computer in his haste to grab the remote, barely catching the laptop before it hit the floor. The sudden movement must have startled Garth because he puffed up his chest and crowed at Dez before awkwardly flying to land on the couch behind me.

Dez ignored the angry rooster and turned on the flat screen monitor. A few seconds later, we were all looking at the video frame of Robert Thompson from the day he dropped deadly magic in Monty Corville's pool. Dez zoomed in on his arm. "What if this isn't a tattoo? What if it's a demon mark?"

I grabbed Dez and planted a kiss in the middle of his forehead. "You're a genius."

"According to my IQ, that is correct," he agreed with a cheeky grin.

"Max, we could really use that demon sigil book from your library," I said.

Bea jumped to her feet. "No need. We already have one here." She crossed the room to the magical library corner she'd been organizing this week. She sat the crystals and the Ouija board on the floor, so she could dig through the stack of books beneath them. "Here's one!" She waved a thick volume bound in leather and then pulled out a second book. "And two." She carried the books back to the couch and sat between Helen and me.

Because we only had a partial image from the video still, it was difficult to match it to a sigil. When it was apparent that this would take a while, Dez volunteered to go pick up pizzas, so we didn't have to deactivate the wards for a delivery guy.

Bea, Helen, and I spent the next twenty minutes hunched over books searching for a match, noting any that resembled the partial mark visible on Thompson's arm. I handed the book I was looking through to Helen and stood up to pace the floor. "I don't see any that are a clear match." It's possible that the mark was a tattoo after all, but Dez's theory made too much sense to dismiss that easily. The demon's sigil was required for a summoning. Although a sharpie would work in a pinch, tattooing or carving the sigil into the host was a common method.

Tired of sitting on the sidelines, Volkov got to his feet. "I have a few rare reference tomes in my library that have lesser-known demon marks. I need to grab some clothes and personal items anyway, so I'll bring the books back with me."

I felt a twinge of guilt when I remembered his mother was visiting. "You don't have to come back tonight, you know. We'll keep searching through these, and you can call if you find anything."

"I'm coming back." His tone didn't invite argument. "But feel free to eat your greasy pizza without me. I'll grab real food."

Nash grunted. "Your loss, man."

When Dez got back with the pizzas, we took a research break to eat. With our stomachs full, we gave the search one last try, going through several other books Bea grabbed from the corner stash.

"This is hopeless," I said, tossing the book I'd just searched on top of our growing reject pile. "Hopefully, Max had better luck."

Nash stood to stretch his legs. Before he sat back down, he stopped to stare at Garth. "Something is seriously wrong with that rooster."

Garth stood over the Ouija board, nudging the planchette with his little foot. Once he saw he had our attention, Garth crowed triumphantly.

"Will you look at that?" Helen exclaimed. "What a smart boy he is."

Nash mumbled something under his breath, prompting a new round of outraged crowing.

Helen jabbed her good elbow into Nash's side. "Behave."

"Me?" Nash said. "What about that feathered menace? He's the one destroying your game board."

I closed my eyes and pinched the bridge of my nose, anticipating the lecture that was coming.

"Game board?" Helen put her good hand on her hip and, because she only stood four foot ten inches, stared up at Nash. "That board is most certainly not a game. It is a powerful divination tool and a communication conduit for spirits. Game board," she muttered, shaking her head.

Nash stared down at Garth, who appeared smug as Helen chewed his owner out. "Oh, of course. I suppose the rooster is communicating with his ancestors over there."

Garth locked his beady red eyes on Nash and nudged the planchette onto the K. When Helen cooed over his accomplishment, he moved it again, stopping on the I. By the third letter, we were all crowded around the board watching the rooster. I grabbed a pen and wrote the letters on my hand as Garth selected them. After moving the planchette several more times, he ended on the S. Then Garth puffed up his chest and crowed before marching off the Ouija board.

Everyone turned to me, and I held up my hand that spelled K-I-M-A-R-I-S.

We were still staring at the word when Volkov returned, holding an old book in his hand. "Dez was right. It is a sigil," he announced to the quiet room.

No one breathed as we waited for the name.

Volkov held the book open to show us a familiar image.

"It's the sigil for a powerful war demon named Kimaris. If the accounts in this book are true, he has the ability to turn shadows into weapons. He's also known for hunting lost things."

We all looked over at Garth who had his beak buried in Dez's leftover Bloody Mary that had been spiked generously with O positive.

CHAPTER 26

Nash crossed himself and backed away from the chicken. "I told you that was a demon rooster."

Helen swatted him on the back of the head. "Just because he associates with demons doesn't make him bad."

Nash sputtered, his eyes flicking between the angry witch and the gloating rooster. Bea, Dez, and I were still too shell-shocked to speak.

Volkov closed the book. "Do I want to know?"

I pointed to the word on my palm. "Garth identified our demon with that Ouija board."

Volkov snapped his mouth closed and stared at Garth along with the rest of us.

Helen crouched down next to Garth and petted his sapphire blue feathers while making soothing sounds. "You don't listen to Nash. You're still my good boy." The rooster preened under Helen's praise, and then struck out with his left spur, catching Nash on the shin before he could scramble out of his reach.

"Ow!" Nash grumbled.

"Do you have a name, hon?" Helen asked the rooster.

We all watched as he spelled G-A-R-T-H.

"Holy shit!" Volkov staggered back a step. "You weren't kidding."

"Who could make this up?" I might regret it, but I had to ask. "Garth, do you have a demon in there?" I tapped his little chest.

Garth moved the planchette to yes and watched me expectantly, waiting for the inevitable next question.

"Can you tell us your demon's name?" I held my breath. *It was probably some harmless, low-level demon,* I assured myself. After all, he was currently bonded to a rooster. *How bad could it be?*

Garth took his time moving the planchette, and I wrote his answer on my palm. A-N-D-R-A-S.

Nash snatched the book out of Volkov's hand and searched for the name. When he found the entry, his eyes widened. "Well, that's just great." He glared at me and pitched his voice higher in a terrible impression of mine. "He'll be good for you, you said. He can be your emotional support chicken."

I flinched. "That's not exactly what I said. I told you pets were good for ex-soldiers." The research backed me up on that.

"Sure," Nash agreed, placing his hand over his heart like he was about to say the pledge. "Andras and I can bond over our war experiences."

"He's a war demon, too?" I asked. That was bad news. If he and Kimaris were on the same side, we'd essentially have a spy amongst us. Granted, he couldn't exactly give away our secrets in his current form. I stared at the board. *Unless he spelled them out.*

Nash shoved the open book into my hands. "No. Worse."

What could be worse than a war demon?

Bea scootched in, so she could read over my shoulder. "Oh my." She fanned herself.

"What?" Volkov snapped.

I cleared my throat and read the entry out loud. "Andras is a vengeance demon." That was better than a war demon. "Back in his home realm," I said, diplomatically avoiding calling it hell since I didn't want to offend him. "Andras commands thirty legions of demons and is fond of riding on a strong, black wolf." I winked at Volkov. *Sweet.*

Helen nodded. "I saw the leadership potential right away."

Nash made a choking sound in his throat, but Helen ignored him.

I kept reading. "Andras has a reputation for stirring up trouble." That did sound like him. "He's said to be extremely dangerous and volatile." When I glanced down at Garth, he hopped from foot to foot like he was nervous. Poor little guy was probably afraid we wouldn't like him now that we knew he had a demon inside. I scanned the page until I hit on something positive. "Oh, well this is nice. It says here that he teaches those he favors to disembowel their enemies."

"So nice," Nash yelled, stalking over to the bar and grabbing the whiskey bottle. He didn't even bother pouring a shot, just tipped it back and took a long swig.

"It could be worse," Bea said. "I'm glad he's on our side."

"Is he?" Nash asked, taking a longer pull on the bottle.

I shrugged. "He hasn't murdered you in your sleep, so he must be fond of you." Garth was just high-strung. If he had wanted to harm us, he had plenty of opportunities. Bea was right. There were worse things than having a vengeance demon on your side.

Helen held out her good arm, and Garth hopped on like a

trained hawk. She shot Nash her disappointed look. "You listen up, young man. Until you cool off and are ready to be kind, Garth is coming home with me. Get your shit together. You have responsibilities now." Before Nash could argue, Helen turned to Bea. "Get the cage. I'm tired. We're going home."

Once the shock wore off, the rest of us stayed up for hours going over intel and the angles. There was only so much heist planning you could do across state lines though. At the end of the night, we decided to leave for Nebraska in the morning. I texted the girls with the update and confiscated Nash's truck keys. Half a bottle of whiskey put him firmly in need of a designated driver. After grudgingly agreeing to let Nash sleep it off in his guest room, Dez buckled him in the passenger seat of his tiny smart car and drove home.

"You sure you want to stay?" I asked Volkov, giving him an out. One night on an uncomfortable air mattress was torture enough. I wouldn't blame the man if he went home to his Egyptian cotton sheets and luxury bathroom.

He reeled me in for a kiss. "I'm sure."

"What about your mother?" I kept my voice neutral.

"She told me about the lunch." Volkov peered down at me. "And I asked her to leave."

Part of me was relieved, but I also felt bad that I was the reason for the rift. "You didn't have to do that. In her own way, she's trying to look out for you."

Volkov dropped his forehead to mine. "My relationship with my mother is complicated, but she doesn't know me as well as she thinks she does."

He'd changed when he went home to grab the reference books, and the soft cotton of his t-shirt invited my touch. I spread my palms across his chest and leaned in, brushing my lips over his in a sweet kiss. "It was nice that she came to visit," I said.

"She comes this time every year even though I tell her not to."

I was close enough to feel the slight tremor that ran through his body when he said it, and another piece clicked into place. "This is the time of year you lost your sister, isn't it?"

He swallowed. "Yes."

Suddenly, the fall performance date for The Nutcracker made perfect sense. He timed it each year to commemorate Anya's short life. I wrapped my arms around his waist and squeezed. We stood together for a long time.

When we finally broke apart, I met his eyes. "It's our last night before I head out on another job. What do you want to do?" Last night, I passed out as soon as my head hit the over-inflated air mattress. Tonight, I was determined to be better company.

Volkov's gaze heated, dipping to my lips and then lower. "There's one thing I've wanted to do since you were in Los Angeles."

"Oh yeah?" Hooking my fingers through the loops of his jeans, I pulled his body flush against mine. I hoped he wanted to try out some of those fancy stunt moves because I was definitely up for one-on-one grappling. "What's that?"

He bent his head and whispered in my ear. "Tell me you kept that cheerleading outfit."

I laughed. "I'm always up for a little role playing, but I'm afraid that cheer costume stayed on set."

Volkov groaned, a sound I wanted to inspire again tonight. "Even the eagle underwear?" he asked.

I leaned back, sure that he must be joking, but the fire in those eyes was all for me. “You’re serious?”

“Yes.” He captured my lips in a scorching kiss, tugging on the bottom one with his teeth. “That picture Kali sent to the group chat was hot as hell.”

I couldn’t help the laugh that bubbled up. “You know,” I teased. “If you liked those eagle bloomers, I have a pair of granny panties you’re going to find so hot.”

Instead of laughing with me, he growled and palmed my ass, lifting me until I obliged by wrapping my legs around him. He backed me into the wall, his lips teasing the column of my neck, the hard length of him pressed against my core proving that sexy lingerie was vastly overrated.

CHAPTER 27

Helen's face was the first thing I saw when I woke, and it took me several seconds to remember where I was. Volkov had been called out on pack business shortly before dawn, so I was sleeping alone. Or at least I had been until Helen barged in beeping like a human alarm clock. When I didn't immediately get up, she pulled the plug on the air mattress, and it deflated rapidly.

"Why?" I whined like a teenager.

Volkov and I hadn't done much sleeping last night, and I was bone tired. I rolled on my side despite the hard floor and pulled the blanket over my head, hoping Helen would give up and go home.

She nudged me with the toe of her orthopedic sneaker. "You better get yourself up right now unless you want to spend the next three years jumping through Martha's hoops like a trained poodle."

I sat up and rubbed the sleep out of my eyes. "What are you talking about?"

"I've got a mole on the inside," Helen said like that explained everything.

"A mole?" I stood up and stretched.

"Yeah." Helen shoved a duffle bag in my arms and slapped me on the butt. "Come on. We need to hustle before Martha gets here with her goon squad."

"Why is Martha coming here?"

Helen tapped her foot impatiently while I pulled on ripped jeans and put on a bra and fresh t-shirt. "She got an emergency containment order from the Witches' Council for you."

I scraped my hair into a low ponytail, securing it with a hair band.

"What? Why?" According to Sato, I had a temporary reprieve until this job was done. Why on earth would Celeste act without the Enclave's approval? I ducked into the small bathroom and quickly brushed my teeth, leaving the door open, so I could hear Helen's answer.

"She used that explosion as her excuse. Martha claimed you caused it with a spell gone wrong, said you were a danger to yourself and others." Helen scoffed. "I didn't think she'd stoop so low, but maybe she is the one who set off that bomb."

How convenient for Martha. As soon as I came out of the bathroom, Helen handed me my shoes and motioned for me to hurry up.

After grabbing my leather jacket, I searched the warehouse for my phone. "Where's your sling?" I asked Helen, noting that both her hands were free.

"Psssh. I don't need it. I took a healing potion when I got home. Good as new." She rotated her shoulders to prove her point. Then she went back to pacing the room while I searched for my phone, her head swiveling at every slight noise.

I narrowed my eyes. "Did you put the healing potion in an energy drink again?"

Helen found my phone and tossed it to me, not answering my question. "You could use a little pep in your step yourself. Now, let's go."

I followed her down the stairs. "Where is everyone else?"

"Bea has the car idling on the curb for a quick getaway. Nash and Dez are going to meet us outside of town when we ditch those busybody witches. Janis is chicken-sitting," she said. "I sent Volkov a message, but he hasn't responded yet."

"And you're sure Martha is on her way?"

Helen didn't need to answer because as soon as we stepped out of the building, Martha pounced. Two of her stockier witches came at me from either side of the door, taking me by surprise when they slammed me against the brick building and slapped magic-canceling handcuffs on my wrists. After a scuffle in which Helen landed a couple good blows to the kidney, Martha put a second set of magic-canceling handcuffs on Helen.

"Leave her out of it," I snarled, kicking out a leg and connecting with Martha's thigh before she limped out of striking distance.

"Stop that," she ordered.

"Then let Helen go."

"Absolutely not." Martha straightened her navy blazer and glared at me. "She is interfering with a lawful arrest."

"You're not a sheriff, Martha. You can't arrest people." Helen rattled her cuffs. When Martha tried to grab her arm, Helen snapped her teeth, narrowly missing a finger. At the outraged expression on Martha's face, I laughed.

"Oh, you think that's funny?"

"It's pretty funny." I probably should have been taking this whole thing more seriously, but I was operating on three hours of sleep and an empty belly. Plus, Helen kept baring her teeth at Martha like a feral cat hyped up on caffeine and ginseng.

Before Martha could corral either of us, Bea gunned the engine of Helen's station wagon and threw open the passenger side door like she was auditioning for getaway driver. "Get in!" she yelled. Despite it being barely past seven in the morning, Bea was wearing skin-tight leopard print pants, a low cut top, and sky high teased bangs.

Martha body blocked the escape route, darting back and forth to prevent Helen from making a break for the car. Watching this play out, I sincerely doubted Martha was capable of planting that bomb.

"Are you seeing this?" I asked the witches who each had one of my arms in a firm grip. This was the most absurd arrest attempt I'd ever witnessed, and I grew up in a house full of thieves, so I'd seen my share of takedowns. God, I hoped Dez had put up that security camera we'd talked about, so there would be footage of this.

Volkov must have checked his messages because he parked his Audi behind Helen's station wagon and stalked toward us, murder in his eyes. "What the fuck do you think you're doing, Martha?"

Martha backed up when he kept coming, looking at the two witches holding me for aid. When she realized there was no escape, Martha planted her feet and set her padded shoulders. "I have authorization to take her in."

"From whom?" Volkov demanded.

Martha lifted her chin. "The Witches' Council."

Volkov smiled. "They have no jurisdiction over Riley."

Martha waved a piece of paper under Volkov's nose. "This says otherwise."

"Can I see it?" he asked reasonably. When she handed it over, Volkov ripped it into pieces and tossed it over his shoulder. "I don't care what that said. You have no authority here." He turned to the two witches gripping me by the arms. "You have until I count down from three to release her. If I get to one, and your hands are still on her, I will remove them from your bodies."

Because I was sandwiched between the two witches, I could feel the terror make their hands tremble and their breath quicken.

"Three," Volkov started.

Neither witch risked a count of two, dropping their hands and scrambling away from me.

Volkov jerked his head toward the idling car. "Go," he told me.

I moved closer to Helen, but she stopped me with a shake of her head. "I'll be fine, hon. You go. Remember what I told you. Trust your instincts, and you'll be fine."

"I will," I promised. Before joining Bea in the car, I paused long enough to give Volkov a kiss on the cheek. When he glared down at the handcuffs still on my wrists, I winked. "I'll hold on to these. They'll make for even better role playing than that cheerleading outfit."

He maintained his glower for the witches, but there was a hint of heat as he watched me go. I put a little extra sass in my walk for him. When I reached the station wagon, I slid into the passenger seat.

Helen hollered at Bea before I pulled the door closed. "You watch her back."

Bea nodded and then hit the gas, channeling Helen's

defensive driving skills as she raced beyond Martha's reach. When we got to the meetup point, Nash and Dez were waiting with a bag full of breakfast burritos and a full tank of gas in our D&R Cleaning van. Despite his obvious hangover, Nash took the driver's seat over Bea's objection, relegating her to shotgun. Dez climbed in the back with me. I made quick work ditching the cuffs before grabbing a breakfast burrito for each hand and settling in for the ride to Nebraska.

CHAPTER 28

There were a million ways Dez could nerd out, but military history wasn't one of them. That was why an hour into the drive, Dez took over driving duties, so Nash and I could plan how to get into that missile silo. Because the back of our van was kitted out with a row of monitors and high-tech gear, Nash pulled up satellite imaging on one monitor and the silo blueprints on another.

"How does someone just buy a military silo?" I asked Nash, who was studying the monitors intently, his hangover mostly forgotten.

"The military decommissioned a lot of them in the 1960s and sold off a bunch." Nash tapped the satellite image of our site. "This one housed an Atlas missile. There were only seventy-two of them built." He pointed at the blueprints. "Although there were a few configurations, this one stored the missile vertically in an underground silo. They were designed to lift the missile to the surface for launch. Because the silo on this one is vertical, it's over a hundred feet deep and connects via tunnel to a launch control center. That's likely where the

Thompsons will be. People often renovate these and turn the command center into living space."

I studied the monitors and pointed to the large doors embedded in the ground that seemed like the logical access point. "Can we go through these?" According to the blueprints and diagrams, those blast doors led into the silo itself. Since the Thompsons would be in the command center, we could easily rappel into the silo and attack via tunnel. They'd likely have wards and magical booby traps of course, but I could walk right through them.

"Not happening," Nash said. "Those doors weigh at least eighty tons and are three or four feet thick."

I whistled. "Then how do we get in."

He pointed to the concrete door leading to the command center. "The easiest way is always through the front door."

"So what are you suggesting? We knock and wait for Robert Thompson to roll out the welcome mat?"

Nash flicked me an annoyed look. "No. One option is to Trojan horse our way inside. This guy is a prepper, or at least he was before he turned into a blood sucker." Dez grumbled from the front seat, but Nash ignored him. "Dez said Thompson gets regular deliveries of bulk food and water to the silo location. The water comes in fifty-five gallon barrels, and they arrive like clockwork every month. We could drain one, put a false bottom on, and smuggle you inside that way."

I grinned. I'd never tried to pull a Trojan horse before. "I like it. When is the next delivery?"

Nash grimaced. "A week from today."

"That's too long," I said. No way we could leave that book in their hands another week, not to mention hiding out in a small town without drawing attention was virtually impossible. "What's Option B?"

He zoomed in on the satellite image and pointed to a spot close to the blast doors. "I've been studying the site. This metal grate covers an air vent that leads directly into the silo. Back when this was an active missile site, they would've had armed guards to secure it. I doubt Thompson has given it much thought. It'll be bolted down, but all we'd need is a bolt cutter to get in. Then you could rappel down to the mezzanine below, and from there, make your way to the tunnel leading to the command center."

We had our way in. Any option that included rappelling in like an action hero was a winner in my book. I held out my hand for a fist bump. Nash stared at it, shook his head, and then looked back at the monitors.

"Come on." I nudged his arm. "You can't still be mad about Garth."

He grunted. *I guess he could.* By the end of this job, he'd be over his snit. Nothing brought a team together like infiltrating an underground bunker for the greater good.

"Dez," I called to the front. "Did you keep that rappelling equipment in here?"

"Of course."

"Then that's our way in," I said. "Hey Dez, the next decent-sized town you pass through, find us a hardware store." This part of the state had more sorghum fields than stoplights, so it would be another hour before we hit a town big enough to have a hardware store.

We spent the drive time cataloguing the types of attacks the Thompsons might throw at us. "Alright," I said. "As an air elemental, Phoebe will most likely have complex wards set around the property. Those won't be an issue for me, but they'll keep Dez and Bea at a distance." I studied Nash. "There's a good chance that the wards won't work on you.

Correct me if I'm wrong, Bea, but most witches set wards to be triggered by either supernaturals or humans, right?"

"That's right," Bea agreed. "Usually, if they want to ward against both, they layer two together."

"Most vampires view humans as blood donors—no offense, Dez—not threats. From what we know, the demon Robert Thompson is hosting is a big-shot war demon. He's likely to view humans as even less of a threat than most vampires would. Plus, the Thompsons get regular deliveries, so I doubt they've set wards to keep humans out."

"Good," Nash said. "You'll need backup on the ground." He gestured toward the land surrounding the missile silo. "They're on five acres. From Robert's online posting history, I gather he was about as paranoid as they come. We already know he has a stockpile of weapons, including semi-automatic rifles and plenty of ammo. We should also assume that he's rigged up some nasty surprises on that land."

"Like what?" Bea asked, pivoting in her seat to frown at us.

"Land mines possibly, trip wires and cameras for sure."

I nodded. I'd assumed as much. "Don't worry, Bea. You'll be far away from the action."

"It's not me I'm worried about." She chewed on her bottom lip.

I pointed to myself. "Null, remember?"

Bea didn't look any less worried. "Yeah, well tossing bricks at your head with a gust of wind will knock you out just like anyone else."

She had a point. "I'll do my best to take her out first." Should that fail, I had pretty decent reflexes to help me dodge bricks.

Bea twisted a lock of dyed blonde hair around her finger, looking more agitated by the second. "I don't like that you're going in alone to face a powerful demon and an elemental who already knows magic doesn't work on you."

I couldn't argue the point because I'd seen the flash of recognition in Phoebe's expression when her magic had no effect on me at Corville's house. "I'll be fine," I assured her.

"Have you considered that she might not set normal wards?" Bea asked. "She's an air elemental with a talent for altering spells. She could use that to set up magical booby traps. You could set off a regular tripwire that she's connected a spell to that triggers all sorts of attacks."

Bea was getting herself more worked up as she talked. Unlike Helen who turned into a general at the first sign of trouble, Bea was a worrier. I cut our what-if conversation short and did my best to soothe her fears. A few minutes later, Dez parked in front of a hardware store, so Nash could buy bolt cutters.

"Grab some salt while you're in there," I called after Nash. I had no idea if a salt circle could be used to trap a vampire, but since I knew his demon's name and sigil, it was worth a shot.

"I need to use the bathroom." Bea opened her door. Because those leopard print pants were far too tight for pockets, she tucked her cell phone into her ample cleavage and got out of the van.

"Do you want me to go with you?" I asked.

"No. I need a minute to myself," she said without looking at me.

Bea made it back to the van first, looking less tense than when she had before. Nash opened the van door and climbed in, carrying several bags along with the bolt cutters.

"You got the salt?"

He rummaged in the bag and pulled out a large bag of canning salt. "It was this or tiny salt and pepper shakers."

"That'll work." *Maybe.* I eyed his haul. "Tell me you got snacks." I peered inside when he set the bags down to close the door. "What's all this?" It certainly wasn't snacks. He'd bought fertilizer, a small can of butane, some steel pipe, and a scented candle.

"A pipe bomb makes a pretty good distraction," he said.

Bea turned in her seat to glare at Nash. "Haven't we had enough explosions for one week?"

At the mention of the apartment explosion, I stared down at his supplies. "People use fertilizer to make IEDs, right?"

"Yeah," Nash confirmed. "Paired with fuel and a detonator, ammonium nitrate fertilizer is a common ingredient. Why?"

"Because when I broke into coven headquarters, I found an invoice for bulk fertilizer." Maybe I'd been too quick to dismiss Martha as annoying but harmless.

"It's possible, I guess, that Martha used that fertilizer to make the IED in your apartment building," Bea conceded. "But it's equally likely that she ordered it for the coven garden."

Whatever Martha used it for was a worry for another day. Dez pulled onto a gravel road that would take us to the Thompson property. I set aside my suspicions for now and focused all of my attention on the job at hand.

CHAPTER 29

After Nash decked himself out in camo face paint, he left to map out potential threats on the land surrounding the silo and to dismantle as many as he could. The rest of us huddled in the van watching footage from Dez's drone. Bea had spelled it to be both silent and invisible, which allowed Dez to fly it everywhere without alerting the Thompsons to its presence.

We'd been at the surveillance for a couple hours before I needed to stretch my legs. Nash came up behind me without a sound, making me jump two feet in the air when he tapped my shoulder. I clutched my hand to my racing heart. "Gee, Nash. You almost gave me a heart attack."

"Occupational hazard." He didn't sound sorry. Nash's hazel eyes scanned the area around the van, and he kept his voice hushed despite the quarter mile between us and the silo.

Dez had parked the van behind some trees in a field after Nash used his new bolt cutters to cut the chain on the gate. I'd left a twenty-dollar bill lying on the ground under the chain to alleviate my guilt.

I stretched my arms over my head and bent my knees to keep them limber. "You find a good route?"

"If we approach from the north, we'll have tree cover most of the way. There's a good spot for me to hunker down with a rifle and the pipe bomb."

"You brought a rifle?"

Nash gave me an are-you-for-real look. "Of course, I did."

"Okay." I held my hands up. "But you know you can't kill a vampire with a bullet, right?"

Nash grunted. "I can take out his kneecaps though, or shoot for the eyes."

"Yikes. Remind me to stay on your good side." He arched a brow, and I slugged him on the arm. "Stop being such a grouch about that rooster. How was I supposed to know he had a vengeance demon in him?"

Nash rubbed the spot I hit. "Oh, I don't know, maybe look into those evil red eyes?"

Dez opened the van door and motioned us inside before I could argue for Garth's finer qualities. "There's a car headed this way," Dez said.

The county road we were on was poorly maintained with few houses along it to draw traffic. In the two hours we'd been parked here, we'd only seen one old farm truck drive down it. I ducked my head as I climbed into the back of the van.

"You think it's the farmer who owns this field?" I asked, crossing my fingers and hoping it was anyone else. Our presence would be hard to explain, even if we hadn't cut the chain off his gate.

"Nah," Dez said. "It's not a pickup." He pointed to a monitor that showed his footage from the drone as he flew it above the road.

The vehicle coming our way was a compact car with shiny red paint that hadn't seen much gravel-road driving. Nash, Dez, and I all crowded around the monitor, but Bea stayed in the passenger seat glued to her phone.

"Can you get a closer look at the driver?" I asked Dez.

He obliged, flying the drone close enough we could see the face of the woman driving the car. She appeared to be in her mid to late thirties, with short dark hair, funky glasses, and a sour expression. "She looks city through and through. What's she doing out here?"

Bea cleared her throat. "Don't be mad."

All three of us turned to stare at her. "Bea," I said. "What did you do?"

She bit her lip. "I called in backup."

My mouth dropped open. "Who?" We were in the middle of nowhere. Who could she possibly know out here?

Bea swallowed and refused to look me in the eye. "I know someone on the Witches' Council."

I made a strangled sound as the magnitude of what she'd just done hit me. "You called the Witches' Council?" I tried and failed to keep my voice from rising. "The same council that just gave Martha the green light to bring me in? That council?"

Bea fidgeted in her seat. "My contact is discreet. She promised not to bring Celeste or the full council in on this."

"When did you call her?" Thinking about it, I realized when she'd done it. "In the bathroom of that hardware store." I glared at her. "And what exactly is this?"

Bea licked her lips and looked out the window toward the road. "My contact arranged for a fire elemental out of Omaha to assist us."

Nash swore. "The last thing we need is an amateur bungling this job."

I dropped my head in my hands until I could get a handle on my temper. "Do you even understand what you've done?" I asked Bea, my voice cracking. I lifted my head. "This witch is not only going to get in the way, she could very easily get me killed."

"No," Bea insisted. "She's here to help."

"I've seen the kind of help the Witches' Council dishes out, Bea, and I want no part of it." I clenched my fists in my lap and breathed through the hurt. "Why would you call them?" Bea hated the suffocating rules and endless power plays as much as the rest of us. I couldn't believe she'd done this.

She stared at the hands clenched in my lap and sighed. "You don't have any magic, Riley. You can't go up against people like this without power of your own."

I rocked back, the words punching straight through my heart. "You think I'm powerless?"

"Now, I didn't say that," Bea said, still not able to meet my eyes.

"Yes. You did."

Out of everyone here, Bea was the optimist, which made the betrayal that much worse. If the woman who'd helped raise me didn't think I was capable enough to handle this, I didn't hold out hope that a fire elemental on the council's payroll would let me do my job. I brushed away a tear from the corner of my eye and threw open the back doors to confront the stranger Bea trusted more than she did me.

An hour later, I was even more livid with Bea. For someone who I'd wager hadn't stolen so much as a piece of gum, Erika had a lot of ideas about how to run this job. Even worse, she had the backing of the Witches' Council, which meant every time I shot down one of her hair-brained ideas, she threatened to call Celeste. Bea had gone quiet after the first threat of tattling. Now that we'd been at this for what felt like an eternity, Bea flinched every time Erika opened her big mouth.

Erika's latest brilliant idea was to suggest calling the local sheriff's department and asking nicely for an escort inside. "We should try the diplomatic route first, and then if that fails, we can consider more extreme avenues," she urged.

I dug my elbow into Nash's side, ignoring his grunt. "Can I talk to you outside, please?"

Erika continued outlining her non-existent plan to Dez and Bea while Nash and I escaped out the back door. I grabbed Nash by the sleeve and pulled him far enough from the van that I was sure Erika couldn't overhear us. "Did you bring zip ties and duct tape?"

Nash smiled. "Why yes, I did."

"Great. I'm going to need to borrow those." I cracked my knuckles and rolled my neck. "Can you distract Erika long enough for me to secure her wrists behind her back?"

"I have a lot more experience with this sort of thing. Shouldn't you distract her while I put the zip ties on?" Nash asked.

"Under normal circumstances, yes." Nothing about this day had been normal though. "But she is a fire elemental. I don't want to risk her drawing on her power and burning you. Me? I'm immune. She can light herself up like an Olympic torch for all I care. I will get those ties on her wrists." I'd enjoy it, too.

Nash's smile widened. "At least let me be the one who duct

tapes that woman's mouth shut before the next asinine suggestion comes out of it."

"Deal." I held up a hand for a fist bump. This time, Nash didn't hesitate. Turns out, dealing with a council witch fast-tracked team bonding even more than going up against the bad guys.

CHAPTER 30

We left a trussed-up Erika in the van with Dez on reluctant guard duty. I was still too angry to speak to Bea, but after spending an hour in Erika's delightful company, I hoped Bea had the good sense not to attempt to free her. Nash and I approached the silo site cautiously, comms in our ears so Dez could communicate any threats he saw through the drone. The area around the silo consisted of overgrown grass and clumps of trees. Dez had hacked into the single security camera aimed at the main concrete entry door. He'd looped in video, so Robert and Phoebe Thompson wouldn't see our approach.

We paused in the treeline to double check our gear. I'd traded my normal fanny pack for a small black backpack that could hold more items. Inside, I had rappelling gear, a bag of canning salt, a homemade pipe bomb, a can of spray paint to draw a sigil, and a few spy gadgets Dez ordered for me. Our original plan had been for Nash to use the pipe bomb to create enough of a ruckus to cover my escape should I need it. However, that plan had relied on stealth and patience.

With a council witch duct taped to the backseat of our van, we couldn't really afford to take our time. I needed to get in and out as quickly as possible before Erika could break free and make good on her threat to call Celeste. Although I'd sent Sato a message warning him of Celeste's interference, the cell reception out here was spotty, and the message failed to send. That meant I was going with straight-up aggression rather than my normal stealth—hence the pipe bomb.

Satisfied that my gear was in order, I patted the demon blade strapped to my thigh and motioned Nash forward. I couldn't manage my usual optimism though, Bea's words worming into my head despite my best attempts to block them out. I took a steadying breath, twisting the silver and copper ring my mother made me around my finger, the cool weight of it grounding me.

At my signal, Nash and I ran together toward the metal grate that lay between us and a fat paycheck. When we were fifty feet from our target, I saw the magic snaking a circle through the grass. I reached for Nash's arm to stop him, but it was too late. He was already to it. I quickly scanned the area around us, searching for projectiles or weapons that could be triggered by crossing this magic, thankful when I saw nothing.

Nash stepped through the ward, only pausing to look back at me when he realized I'd fallen behind. I let out a relieved breath as he cleared it. My theory about the Thompsons' inability to see humans as threats proved true. There was always a security gap, and arrogance seemed to be theirs.

Nash stared at the spot on the ground that still held my attention. "What is it?" he asked.

"There's some kind of ward there." Since I was the only

one who could see the magic, Nash had to take me at my word. "Fortunately, it didn't knock you on your ass."

He nodded, waiting for me to come through. This ward wasn't like any other I'd come across. Instead of the vibrant, pulsing magic I was used to, this magic had an oily black sheen to it, and it writhed on the ground before me like a living thing. The closer I got to it, the faster my pulse raced. I paused and closed my eyes, concentrating on the magic. It was unlike any elemental magic I'd encountered. With a bad feeling in my gut, I stopped with my toe centimeters from the magic.

"Something's wrong," I told Nash. I knelt down to study it and realized what it was. "Blood ward," I whispered. Phoebe must have altered a normal ward with something from that demon spell book, infusing it with blood magic. I had no idea what it did, but I couldn't risk setting it off. "You get that cover off," I told Nash. "I'll be right there."

Because I couldn't trust my null ability to get me through that magic, I turned to a skill far more ingrained. Grabbing a low branch, I pulled myself onto the massive oak tree and started to climb. When I found a sturdy branch that extended past the magic, I tossed my rappelling rope over it and adjusted it until both ends dangled to the ground. Then I gathered the rope on either side of the branch into my hands and slid down it. By the time I'd pulled the rope from the tree, Nash had the metal grate off. After securing my rope and adjusting my backpack, I rappelled into the dark.

Despite wearing my quietest shoes, I landed on the metal mezzanine with a clang. I left the rope where it hung. My plan was to waltz out the front door with that spell book, but climbing my way out was a solid Plan B. I held a small flashlight between my teeth as I navigated through the dark tunnel leading to the command center. That left my hands free to grab the pipe bomb out of my backpack and the lighter out of my pocket.

When I neared the end of the tunnel, I paused to listen. At first, I heard nothing. Then I picked up the low murmur of two distinct voices, which meant they were one elemental short of an apocalypse. *One positive,* I thought. Too bad, it was stacked against a longer list of negatives.

I pulled a periscope out of my backpack and angled it around the corner until I spotted the Thompsons and my target. The vampire and the witch were moving around the space gathering items for something. The spell book was on a pile of maps lying on a table in the middle of the room. I had a clear path to it.

I rolled my shoulders and prepared the bomb, readying to make my big entrance. Once I tossed it, I'd have mere seconds to snatch that book before the Thompsons realized what was happening. I was confident that I could withstand any magic Phoebe hurled at me, but I needed to keep myself out of Robert's reach. I shut down the doubts pinging around in my head and slowed my breathing. One last look, and I'd make my move.

"Shit," I muttered looking through the periscope. Both of them were directly in front of a large map laid out on the table, the demon spell book now in Pheobe's hands. The items they'd gathered were clearly for a spell they were preparing to perform. Her vampire husband watched intently as she flipped through the demon spell book until she located the page she wanted. With everything arranged to her satisfaction, she pulled a small vial out of her pocket.

Her voice rang clearly through the room, the words

sending a chill down my spine. "Sacrifice the child who wields water and air," Phoebe said.

Robert's rough voice followed hers, "Destroy the vessel, weaken the forge."

Phoebe then began chanting and tipped the vial she held, drops of blood hitting the map and lighting it up like a beacon. I gasped. This had to be the blood-tracing spell in action. As the light carved a path through the map, Phoebe paused her chant, and the two of them repeated the words from earlier.

My first thought was that they were using my blood in that tracing spell, but then the words registered, and I knew. They weren't doing that spell to find me. They searched for the child. *Sacrifice the child who wields water and air.* Those were words of prophecy, and my stomach sank as I realized what they meant to do.

CHAPTER 31

Of all the contingency plans, I didn't have one for mid-ritual. I had two choices. I could wait them out and hope this spell didn't lead them to an innocent child, or I could toss my homemade bomb and take my chances. Neither option was good, but only one of them risked a child sacrifice to rip a hole in the veil. There really was no choice.

"Nash," I whispered into the comms. "Can you hear me? I could really use a distraction right about now."

Of course, he couldn't because I was surrounded on all sides by thick concrete walls. I was on my own.

Sometimes, I jinxed myself. As soon as I heard hushed voices coming down the tunnel, I knew this was one of those times. I saw Bea first, Erika following in her wake.

The sight of the two women spurred me into action. I lit the fuse, tossed my bomb, and dove into the fray, demon blade in my hand. The element of surprise got me to the book, and Erika's appearance gave me the distraction I needed to snatch it. Unfortunately, neither gave me enough lead time to make an escape. I tossed the priceless demon artifact across the room, putting me between it and the vampire coming for it. At least, it might buy me some time. When Robert caught sight of my blade, he paled and stopped abruptly, his eyes never leaving it.

"You know what this is, I take it?"

The fact that his gaze never left it was answer enough.

"Then you know this blade can kill a vampire with one strike." Normal blades wouldn't do it, but this one had been forged in hellfire. It was a rare weapon capable of killing demons as well as vampires. With my free hand, I slid the backpack off my shoulder and tossed it toward Bea. "Salt is inside," I yelled.

It took her a second to register what I wanted her to do, but I saw when she figured it out. Bea ducked an air attack Phoebe threw at her and ran for the backpack. Phoebe's second attack landed, and Bea screamed in pain as she hit the floor.

"Erika," I shouted. "Do something!"

Emboldened by my divided attention, Robert edged closer. I slashed the dagger toward his chest, but his reflexes were good enough that he danced out of reach, bloodlust glazing his eyes at my aggression.

Erika stood frozen. I yelled her name again, and that finally snapped her out of her fear. She shook like a leaf, but she stepped up, forming a weak ball of fire in her hands. It was enough to draw Phoebe's attention away from Bea though. While I held Robert temporarily at bay, Bea staggered to her feet. She sliced off a corner from the bag of canning salt and ran a circle around the room, leaving plenty of space to maneuver outside the circle.

When Robert lunged toward her, I darted forward and sliced his thigh. He hissed in pain and turned back to me, giving Bea enough time to finish her circle. She hunted frantically for something to draw the sigil, finally remembering the backpack. Bea found the can of spray paint in the side pocket and, with shaking hands, drew Kimaris' sigil on the floor, closing the circle with salt.

I jumped over the line and waited to see if it would hold. When Robert hit the barrier, he bellowed with rage, but the circle contained him.

"Get the book," I told Bea, pointing to where it landed. "And then get out. Where's Nash?"

"Erika there sealed the only way in with wards," Bea said, her face flushing. "He and Dez can't cross it. If I hadn't snuck past her before they were set, I'd be out there pacing as well."

Erika was a liability. "Go out the front door," I told Bea, gesturing in the other direction. Erika wouldn't have warded that exit. Thankfully, Bea didn't argue.

With Robert trapped inside the salt circle and Bea safely out of harm's way, I turned to the remaining women in time to see Phoebe take Erika out with a strike to the head. Erika was thrown ten feet, her head cracking against the concrete hard enough that she slumped to the ground. Instead of escaping, Phoebe prepared to deliver the killing blow.

I stepped between the women, taking the shot to the chest. I braced my legs and withstood the magic, but Phoebe gathered another blast of air in her left hand, aiming it for the downed council witch. I couldn't shield Erika from attacks from two different directions, and Phoebe was too far away from me to tackle. But I still had a weapon. I fought through the hurricane-force winds, balancing my demon blade. At the first lull, I threw it, and for a second, I thought my blade would strike true.

Phoebe laughed and flicked her wrist, sending the blade

clattering harmlessly to the floor. Then she pulled the air around her and smiled at me, sure that she had me beat.

I had nothing left but my instincts and my promise to Helen to trust in them. I reached for Phoebe's magic, seeing it pulse blue in the air. When it brushed my skin, I concentrated on the buffer between my body and the magic, and then I willed it to recede. Without that protective barrier, I felt the power sink into my skin.

The silver and copper ring on my finger glowed where the magic touched it, the weight of it grounding me. I coiled Phoebe's magic around my fist like a rope. The witch's eyes widened in horror as she felt me pull the magic from her body and absorb it into my own. When there was no power left for her to draw on, Phoebe ran for the exit. I was still buzzing from the power I'd absorbed, unable to react fast enough to intercept her.

Fortunately, Bea was waiting for her with a grudge and a wicked right hook that laid her out. Bea cradled her bruised knuckles against her chest as she beamed at me. "Got her!"

I concentrated on letting go of the borrowed magic. At first, nothing happened, but eventually, it began to seep from my pores and lift from my skin. I watched it turn back into the air Phoebe had drawn upon to create it. Feeling like myself again, I retrieved my blade. Then I rolled up the map still glowing on the table and shoved it in my backpack, not willing to risk it falling into the wrong hands.

"The book?" I asked Bea.

"Nash has it safe and sound." Bea's smile faltered as she looked at me. "I'm sorry, hon. I was wrong to say what I did. I was scared."

"I know." I was still angry with her, but this was the woman who baked me cookies and gave me unsolicited dating advice. I loved her even through my anger, so I dropped an arm around her and steered her to the exit.

Bea looked over her shoulder at the unconscious elemental and back to me again. "What happened back there?"

"I have no idea," I admitted. "But whatever it was, I'm pretty sure I'm not a null."

EPILOGUE

It had taken a week and the bribe of smoked meat and potato salad to lure the full team to headquarters for a formal vote. As official members of the heist crew, Dez, Nash, Helen, and Kali were all present. Because there was no way I could leave out my other three witches, Alyce, Janis, and Bea were ready to cast their ballots as well. And because offending a vengeance demon wasn't a wise life choice, we'd set up the Ouija board on the floor, so Garth could communicate his vote. So far, he seemed more enamored with Kali's pretty pink water bottle than the opportunity to select a headquarters' name.

I peered in the coffee can that held the contenders and was pleasantly surprised to see several folded pieces of paper. "Last chance to submit a name for consideration." I waved the can around, but no one moved to add a last-minute suggestion. "Alright. Here's how this will work. I'll read out the nominations, and Janis will write them on the chalkboard. Once they're all on there, we'll go down the list, and everyone can raise their hand to indicate their vote."

Garth bristled and crowed.

"Except for you, Garth. You can vote yes on the board for your choice," I said. When he settled, I dug in the coffee can for our first contender, which was Cruz & Associates. I hoped that wouldn't be our winner since it made us sound like a law firm. KC Antiquities was next, followed by Naderi Acquisitions, which cleverly smashed the first letters of Nash's and Dez's names with mine.

My contribution, G.O.A.T. went up next. After a few minutes of everyone trying to puzzle it out, Kali finally asked what the acronym stood for. I grinned. "Grabbing Overpriced Artifacts and Titles."

Alyce held up her hand for a high five. "Nice one."

I'd saved Bea's suggestions for last since she had a plethora of them. Although things were still strained between Bea and me, I'd moved past my initial anger. It would take longer than a week for the hurt at her lack of faith in me to fade. I knew she regretted calling in Erika, but that didn't change the fact that she had done it. When I unfolded the stack of suggestions and read them, I couldn't help but smile though. While they all had a word in them worthy of a heist crew name, she'd managed to make every one of them raunchy.

"And finally, we have Bea's colorful nominations. First up is Magic Fingers." Kali giggled, but that was the tamest of the bunch. I called off the remaining names, which included gems such as Booty Snatchers and Pluck & Pull. Lick, Lust, & Larceny had Dez clutching his side from laughing. The names went downhill from there. By the time I read "Kansas City Snatch," everyone was laughing so hard we had to pause to catch our breath. I wiped a tear from my eye and fought for composure. "Ladies and gentlemen, our final contender." I paused for dramatic effect because this baby was the crown jewel of Bea's bawdy brainstorming. "D.I.C. Squad."

Even Nash snort-laughed at that one. "Do I even want to know what that stands for?"

We all turned expectantly to Bea. Today, she was dressed in hot pink pants and a zebra-striped shirt that only showed a hint of cleavage. She looked smug as she told us. "Demon Imports & Consignments."

"Clever," Helen acknowledged.

"We are not calling ourselves the D.I.C. Squad." Nash shook his head. "Why not just call it the full name?"

Bea huffed. "It would hardly be appropriate to put Demon on a sign out front."

Dez rubbed the back of his neck, his face almost as red as his hair as he stared at her. "But you think D.I.C. Squad is fine for a sign?"

Bea nodded solemnly. "Acronyms are all the rage these days."

The vote was close, with Bea, Alyce, Kali, and Garth casting votes for D.I.C. Squad. With five votes from Nash, Dez, Helen, Janis, and me, G.O.A.T. was our winner though. Since Helen collected favors like a mob boss, she promised to have her guy at the sign shop make us a giant headquarters' sign at cost.

With that settled, I left the team to bond over brisket and drinks, while I slipped into the bathroom to change for my date. This time, I'd been smart enough to ask what I should wear. Even though the opening night performance of The Nutcracker was far from the Bolshoi Ballet, Volkov insisted on a formal dress code for all attendees at the event. Instead of answering my question about what I should wear, however, he'd had a royal blue cocktail dress delivered. The dress was exquisite, and it fit like it had been made for me. The material skimmed my body and was gathered at one shoulder, leaving my left shoulder bare. Since most of my jewelry was better suited to a rock concert than a ballet, I chose a simple gold chain.

Once I was dressed, Kali knocked. "You ready for hair and makeup?" She whistled when I opened the door. "That man has good taste. I'll give him that."

Kali spun me in a circle to get the three-sixty-view before getting to work. Since my normal night-out makeup consisted of cherry lip gloss and whatever funky eyeshadow Bea dolled me up with, I let Kali have free rein. She pulled my hair into a French twist and pinned it in place.

"Are you nervous?" she asked as she started on my makeup.

"Weirdly enough, no." Even though I'd never attended a formal event in my life, unless you counted the supernatural auction I went to in order to steal a demon artifact, my nerves were steady.

I'd been surprised when Volkov asked if I'd like to attend opening night with him. He was letting me into a part of his life that was real and raw, something he held separate from even his mother Irina. Despite the party dress and the pretty makeup, tonight wouldn't be a whisk-me-away kind of date like our first one had been. But as sweet as that first date had been—poison ivy aside—tonight was the kind of date that forged a bond that went beyond chemistry and common interests. Volkov was sharing something precious with me.

"All done," Kali announced, handing me a small mirror, so I could see the back of my hair.

I gave her a hug, and she squeezed me back. "It's beautiful. Thank you." It was a bit surreal to see myself in evening wear in the grimy little bathroom mirror. But Kali had done a wonderful job, transforming me into a woman who wouldn't look out of place at a fancy event honoring his sister's memory.

By the time we left the bathroom, Max Volkov was waiting for me. He was dressed in a black tuxedo that molded to his broad shoulders and trim hips. Volkov smiled appreciatively when he got his first full look at me, but there was a sadness in those sharp blue eyes he couldn't quite hide. Tonight would be difficult for him. Not only was this an event meant to honor his sister's dream, but I also knew that tomorrow marked the date of Anya's death. I suspected he'd scheduled the opening tonight because it was the anniversary of the last night Anya could have lived out her dream.

We arrived a few minutes before the ballet began. Volkov guided me to the center of the reserved front row. No one sat on either side of us, but the theatre itself was fuller than I expected. Kauffman Theatre seated well over a thousand, and at least a third of the seats were occupied—every one of the guests dressed in formal wear.

I bent my head to his and whispered, "Wow. I had no idea that a ballet filled a venue like this." When I glanced around, I noticed several familiar faces including the moms I'd spoken to and several shifters from Volkov's pack. "These aren't all parents and family, are they?"

"No," Volkov said. "I send out complimentary tickets to all of my business associates and the pack."

I threaded my fingers through his, squeezing his hand. This man not only paid for the venue and the costumes, he also made damn sure that the theatre was filled. Teagan slid into the seat next to Volkov minutes before the performance started, carrying an enormous bouquet of flowers. "Sorry I'm late boss. The florist botched the order, so I had to call in some favors."

"Thank you," he said, but his attention was riveted on that stage as the lights dimmed around us.

Teagan moved to a seat in the row behind us, leaving Volkov and me alone in the row. I held my breath as the curtain parted and the music wrapped around us. When the dancers filled the stage, I leaned forward in my seat, waiting for a glimpse of the girl who would live Anya's dream this evening. I imagined what Volkov's sister might have looked like gliding across that stage. Although I had never seen a photograph of her, she was a delicate miniature of Irina in my imagination, long limbed elegance and grace.

When the lead dancer took the stage, she was nothing I had expected. Eleven or twelve years old, she still had the full cheeks and rounded belly of a child. She was shorter than the other dancers, her movements too big and out of sync with the perfect choreography all around her. *Was she nervous?* I wondered. *Or had I misidentified the lead?* I watched the lithe dancers, but everyone else faded into the background.

When the lead stumbled, Volkov's grip tightened on my hand. I glanced at him, expecting to see disappointment that the night he'd worked so tirelessly to make perfect—to make worthy of his sister's memory—rested on the shoulders of a nervous young girl stumbling over her steps. The emotions warring on his handsome face bore no resemblance to disappointment. Flashes of grief, yes. But mostly, he watched her dance with a pride that made my heart catch in my chest. I looked back at that young dancer, seeing her the way he saw her. Her face was filled with the kind of joy only a child doing something she loves is capable of.

When he caught me watching him a second later, Volkov

swallowed past the emotion he wore so plainly. Our conversation from the day I heard him play the Waltz of the Flowers rushed back to me.

"Your sister wasn't a good dancer, was she?" I whispered.

"No." His smile was soft and sad. "But love and pride are not the same thing," he said, echoing my own words back to me.

We both turned our full attention back to that stage and to the brave girl who danced because she loved it and because the alpha beside me made it happen. When the performance ended, Volkov was the first to his feet. And when he gave her the bouquet of flowers nearly as big as she was, he whispered something in her ear that made her beam brighter.

Then he stepped out of the spotlight and reached for my hand.

NEXT IN SERIES

Order Now

NOTE TO READERS

If you enjoyed this book, please consider leaving a review or rating on Amazon and/or Goodreads. Your reviews help new readers discover my books and are always appreciated!

If you'd like to be notified of new releases and exclusive content, you can sign up for my newsletter at lamcbride.com/newsletter/ and join my Facebook Readers Group at https://www.facebook.com/groups/lamcbridereaders

ALSO BY L.A. MCBRIDE

Each series can be read independently, but they are set in the same world with some character crossover.

KALI JAMES SERIES

Book 1: Fastening the Grave

Book 2: Threading the Bones

Book 3: Stitching the Talisman

Book 4: Gathering the Dead

RILEY CRUZ SERIES

Prequel: Boneyard Thief

Book 1: Relic Hunter

Book 2: Brimstone Burglar

Book 3: Magic Heist

Book 4: Cursed Vault

ACKNOWLEDGMENTS

A huge thank you goes to my amazing beta reader Krista Walsh, who talked me off ledges and read chapters right up to the deadline. I'm so grateful for my fellow FAKAs who give me advice, cheer me on, and help brainstorm raunchy business names worthy of Bea. Thank you to Janna Ruth who shared that photo of a hell chicken that made me covet a demon rooster of my very own. Special thanks to my husband who insisted he could show our rooster who was boss. Those chase scenes are all you, babe. Thank you to my fabulous ARC team who helps catch those pesky errors that slip past and spreads the Riley love. The biggest thank you goes to my readers, who patiently wait for my stories.

Printed in Great Britain
by Amazon